The Cat Came Back!

Stephanie saw that the cat's claws had gotten stuck in the fine gold links of her necklace.

"Hold on, kitty," she said gently. "I'll help free you."

It was too late, though. The creature had started to panic. Like a wild cat caught in a hunter's trap, she began to snarl and thrash about trying to free herself.

The more the cat thrashed, the tighter the chain was pulled around Stephanie's throat. Finally the cat freed one paw. She raised her claws above Stephanie's head. In a second the cat would slash Stephanie's face!

Books by Lynn Beach

Phantom Valley: The Evil One
Phantom Valley: The Dark
Phantom Valley: Scream of the Cat
Phantom Valley: Stranger in the Mirror
Phantom Valley: The Spell
Phantom Valley: Dead Man's Secret
Phantom Valley: In the Mummy's Tomb

Available from MINSTREL Books

Phantom Valley™

In the Mummy's Tomb

Lynn Beach

A MINSTREL® BOOK

PUBLISHED BY POCKET BOOKS

New York   London   Toronto   Sydney   Tokyo   Singapore

A MINSTREL PAPERBACK *ORIGINAL*

A Minstrel Book published by
POCKET BOOKS, a division of Simon & Schuster Inc.
1230 Avenue of the Americas, New York, NY 10020

ISBN: 0-671-75925-6

First Minstrel Books printing October 1992

10 9 8 7 6 5 4 3 2 1

A MINSTREL BOOK and colophon are registered trademarks
of Simon & Schuster Inc.

Printed in the U.S.A.

In the
Mummy's
Tomb

CHAPTER 1

"**E**ASY, Beulah. No one's going to hurt you. You know I'd never do anything to hurt you, don't you, girl?" Stephanie Markson said gently.

The cream-colored mare tossed her white mane and whinnied softly, as if she were telling Stephanie it was okay to touch her swollen hoof.

Stephanie carefully stroked the injured leg and slowly ran her hand down to the hoof. Then she unwrapped the layers of warm, wet gauze she had put on a few minutes earlier.

Just then she heard sneakers padding over the hard-packed dirt of the Chilleen Academy stable yard. Moments later the freckled face of Laura Hobbes popped up over the stall door. Laura was Stephanie's best friend and roommate.

"Guess what," Laura burst out, pushing her wire-rimmed glasses back up on her nose.

"Shhhhhh," Stephanie said softly. "Beulah's just about to let me take a good look at her hoof. Aren't you, girl?"

The mare neighed.

Stephanie knew that she had a rare gift—she could share thoughts with animals. "Dr. Doolittle," Laura called her, after the famous book character who could talk to animals.

Stephanie loved animals more than anything. She had wanted to bring her cat to Chilleen Academy, but no pets were allowed in the dorms. The only exception was Jason McCormick's Seeing Eye dog, Errol. Not even gerbils or fish. She felt lucky to put in her weekly work hours at the academy stable. The old log building had once been the private stable of the Chilleen family, and it was Stephanie's favorite place on campus.

Stephanie picked up a large set of tweezers.

"Um, Steph? I hate to bother you and your friend here," Laura said, entering the stall, "but guess who's waiting for you back in our room."

"Here," Stephanie directed, as she picked up an electric lantern and swung it toward Laura. "Hold this for me, will you?"

"It's your—" Laura tried again, but Stephanie cut her off.

"Shine it on her foot. I need to see what I'm doing. Steady now. Thanks."

Laura took the lantern and silently watched her friend go to work.

Stephanie held the mare's leg between her knees and poked the hoof with gentle fingers. She had practically grown up in her father's animal hospital. Her father had started letting her help him when she was eight years old. She had been able to calm an injured animal when no one else could.

She could use her father's help today, she thought. Dr. Markson was back home in Seattle, though. The local vet was far away helping a rancher whose horses had hoof-and-mouth disease. Vernon, the stable hand, was in town and couldn't help her either.

Right then, Stephanie was the mare's only hope to feel better.

"Hold still, girl. I've almost got it. You'll feel better when this is all over, believe me. You'll be running around in no time. Just let me do my stuff."

Stephanie let out a soft whistle as she pulled out a six-inch-long splinter and held it up in the beam of light.

"Yikes," said Laura.

"Where did you pick that up?" Stephanie asked.

The mare tossed her head as if to shrug.

Laura lowered the flashlight, looking a little pale.

"So who?" Stephanie asked as she reached for a tube of cream that would prevent infection.

"Who *what?*" Laura said, still staring at the nasty-looking splinter.

Stephanie rolled her eyes. "Who's waiting for me in our room?"

"Oh!" Laura said, brightening. "Libby!"

"My mom? Really? Here? Now? Today!" Stephanie exclaimed. "I thought she was in Tibet!"

"Egypt," Laura corrected. "She just got back. She said she decided to drop in on her way back to Seattle."

Seattle was the home office of *Coaster*, the magazine Libby Markson worked for. She was their star reporter, covering stories on everything from the latest fad in New York City to the oldest turtle in the Galápagos Islands.

When Stephanie was little, before she had started school, her mother used to take her along on many of these trips. Stephanie still had her passport from those days. It was filled with stamps from far-away places like Singapore, Bali, Katmandu, and Kenya.

Stephanie had liked being with her mother, but she wanted to be a normal kid, too. She wanted to live full-time in a normal neighborhood, with normal kids who called their mothers "Mom." Libby had always insisted that Stephanie call her by her first name.

When Stephanie entered first grade, she got her wish. She stayed home with her father and went to a regular school like all the other kids.

Stephanie quickly washed up. Then she left a note

for her friend Ben Smith. He was to look in on Beulah when he reported for work in a half hour. Ben shared Laura's love for adventure and Stephanie's love of horses.

"You'll never guess how Libby got here," Laura said as they followed the path through the woods from the stable back to the dormitory.

"Hang glider?" Stephanie was only half joking. Her mother would try almost anything.

"You're not that far off. Helicopter."

"Helicopter!" Stephanie's green eyes widened. "So *that* was the racket I heard a while ago. Beulah almost kicked down her stall door when she heard it."

Laura nodded, her blond braid bobbing up and down. "She landed right in Clover Meadow."

"What next?" Stephanie asked, grinning.

"Libby Markson has got to be the coolest mother on the entire planet," Laura declared.

The girls raced into the front hall of the academy. The former Chilleen family home was a western-looking three-story wooden building. Even the furniture looked as if it came out of a western movie. Every piece was dark and solid and built to last.

The girls' room was in the old wing, otherwise known as the "haunted wing." Both girls were a little unhappy that they hadn't yet run into a single ghost.

They entered their room to see Libby studying

Stephanie's bulletin board. Stephanie had tacked up photographs, postcards, drawings, and clippings from magazines and newspapers. Each was on her favorite subject: cats.

Libby Markson was wearing a tan jacket over jeans and a T-shirt. On her head she wore her lucky Seattle Mariners' baseball cap. Her lean face was tanned, and her dark hair was tied back in a ponytail.

"Steph!" she shouted.

Stephanie ran into her mother's arms and gave her a big hug.

"Let me look at you!" Libby stepped back to check out her daughter.

"You look terrific. I bet you've grown three inches since Christmas." She chuckled and looked around. "You can sure tell which side of the room is my Stephanie's!"

Stephanie grinned. Her mother was right. It wasn't just the bulletin board that gave it away. Her dresser top was covered with cat figurines. She had about fifty from all over the world.

Not only that, but there were also pictures of cats on the bedspread, cats on the lampshade, cats on the curtains, a cat rug on the floor, and cats on the towels and sheets. Stephanie's favorite cat was on a poster on the ceiling. It was a beautiful photograph of a white Persian cat. The eyes glowed in the dark.

All of Stephanie's friends at Chilleen knew she was

cat-crazy. A lot of them said that, with her long, dark, silky hair, green, upturned eyes, small mouth, and graceful walk, she even *looked* like a cat. A real compliment, Stephanie thought.

"So how was Egypt?" Laura was always the first to ask Libby about her latest trip. Laura worked on the school newspaper and wanted to be just like Libby when she grew up.

"Hot, dusty, incredibly exciting. I'll tell you what," Libby said, glancing at her man's watch, "I have just enough time to take you both out to lunch. I hear Benny's Hamburger Heaven makes a great bacon cheeseburger. I'll tell you all about Egypt, and give Stephanie her present."

"Present!" Stephanie loved any gifts her mother brought her. "What is it? Tell me what it is!"

"What, and spoil the surprise?" Libby teased. "I'll give it to you in the restaurant—*after* dessert."

Stephanie suddenly remembered something. "I'm supposed to meet Ben at the stables," she said, disappointed.

"Bring Ben along, too," Libby said.

"I have a music lesson," Laura said glumly.

"Change it," Stephanie said. "Your teacher will understand. How often does Libby Markson drop in out of the sky?" She grinned at her mom, then opened her closet to choose some clean clothes.

Just then the room filled with a beeping noise.

"What's that?" Laura asked, frowning. "The fire alarm?"

"Not quite," Stephanie said. "That's Libby's beeper."

Libby dove for the battered canvas bag that had been around the world at least three times. She pushed the button down on her beeper and said, "Someone's trying to get in touch with me. Where's the phone?"

"Down the hall. Near the stairs. I'll show you," Laura said, eager to help.

Libby was back in a few minutes. Her face was flushed and her eyes were shining. Stephanie knew that look all too well.

"Sorry, girls, but I'm afraid we'll have to have lunch some other time," Libby said.

Stephanie was used to the quick changes in plans. The sudden comings and goings at all hours. The phone calls in the middle of the night. It was one of the reasons she had agreed to go to boarding school. Her mother's beeper and her father's beeper might go off at any time. She preferred to live beeper-free at Chilleen.

"That was my editor calling from Seattle," Libby explained breathlessly. "It seems there are a couple of gray whales stuck between some icebergs in a bay in northern Alaska.

"A group of Inuits, a fleet of fishing boats, the National Guard, and a troop of Cub Scouts are all trying to set them free," continued Libby. "It's the kind of news story that people can't get enough of. And it's mine. *If* I can get up there to cover it in time. They've already booked me a flight, so I've got about three seconds to spare."

Stephanie was happy for her mom, but sometimes she wished things didn't change so easily with her. She shrugged and said, "Come on, Laura, let's walk Libby to her chopper."

On the way to the meadow, Libby gave Stephanie her present. It was a small, square package, wrapped in wrinkled blue tissue paper.

"Open it!" Laura said eagerly.

Stephanie pulled back the paper to find a small gray box. Inside the box, nestled in brown crushed velvet, was a necklace. A charm made from dark green stone was hung from a fine gold chain.

"Oooooh!" Laura said, peering closely at it. "What is it?"

"It's Egyptian," Libby explained.

"What are those little marks all over it?" Stephanie wanted to know.

"That's ancient Egyptian writing. You know, hiero-glyphs, the pictures and symbols the Egyptians used for writing. Don't ask me what it all means. But it's pretty, isn't it? Unusual."

"It's beautiful!" Stephanie said, still staring at it. "Is it very old?"

Libby shook her head. "No, it's only a copy of a five-thousand-year-old piece. I found it in a shop in the old section of Cairo. The shopkeeper said these necklaces are very popular. When you wear it, it will ward off the Evil Eye."

At those words, Stephanie felt a sudden chill run up her spine.

Libby's helicopter was sitting in the middle of Clover Meadow, like some giant insect. The pilot was sitting beside it in a folding chair reading the newspaper. He wore mirrored sunglasses and a battered leather flyer's jacket.

Libby called out to him. "Start up the engine, Hank. You've got to buzz me over to the nearest airport so I can catch a flight to Alaska . . . !"

Before the girls knew it, Libby was saying goodbye.

"Thanks for stopping by. Thanks for *almost* taking us out to lunch," Stephanie said. "And thanks for the necklace."

"It looks great on you," Libby said, tousling her daughter's hair. She turned to Laura.

"Take care of my girl for me, will you?" she said.

"Will do," said Laura, her eyes shining in admiration. "Write a great story."

Libby ran in a crouch beneath the blur of the rotor blades, one hand on her lucky baseball cap.

The girls watched, their hair whipped by the wind of the whirling blades. The helicopter lifted off, and hovered just over their heads. Libby waved down to them, then gave them the thumbs-up sign.

The girls watched the helicopter disappear, then Stephanie heaved a deep sigh. "Well! Off she goes!" She fingered the charm around her neck. "Into the wild blue yonder."

"Into wild blue adventure, you mean," Laura said glumly, tugging at her braid. "And off we go, back to our dull lives."

Stephanie had the oddest feeling that her friend was about to be proven wrong. Dead wrong.

CHAPTER 2

"**Y**OU are the luckiest girl at Chilleen," Laura said after lunch as she and Stephanie walked away from the dorm.

Laura was on her way to her music lesson, and Stephanie was going to study math with Ben at the stables. Stephanie and Ben's dislike for math was almost as strong as their love of horses. The faster they studied, the sooner they could saddle up and go for a ride.

"I don't think I'm so lucky," Stephanie said. "I've got a math test this week. I call that bad luck, if you ask me."

"That's not what I mean," said Laura. "You're lucky because your mother flies all over the world and because she brings you interesting gifts from faraway places. She's got such a great job.

"I mean," Laura went on, "how does my mother travel? In a station wagon. What kind of presents does she give me? Banana nut bread that arrives here squished flatter than a pancake. And what kind of career does she have? She teaches the flute to grade school kids. I call that boring—with a capital *B*."

"What's wrong with the flute? You play it, don't you?" asked Stephanie.

"Only because it would break my mother's heart if I didn't," Laura muttered.

Something small and sleek and black shot across the path, startling them both.

"What in the world . . . ?" Stephanie whispered.

"That was either the world's smallest panther or seven years bad luck," Laura replied.

"Only if you're superstitious," Stephanie said. "Look!" she exclaimed. "There she is!"

Stephanie pointed into the bushes in front of a pine tree just off the path. Two round eyes glittered out at them, hard and unblinking.

"It's just a little old black kitten," Stephanie said softly. "She's pretty, isn't she?"

Laura groaned. "Come on, Steph. You've got studying to do. And I've got a lesson."

Stephanie was already kneeling in front of the bush with her hand out. "Here, kitty, kitty, kitty. Come here, pretty kitty. Come to Steph now."

The kitten shrank back farther into the bushes and hissed.

"Leave it alone, Dr. Doolittle," Laura said. "Maybe it's got rabies. You never know."

"She looks healthy to me. Just a little spooked," Stephanie said, her eyes never leaving the cat. "Isn't that true, gal?"

"How do you know it's a girl?"

"It *looks* like a girl. So small and delicate," said Stephanie.

"She's probably starving to death and mean," Laura said, tugging nervously at her braid.

"Somehow I don't think so. Her coat's really shiny. How did you get here, kitty? Don't you know there are no kitties allowed on campus? Do you want to get in trouble with Mrs. Danita?"

"I know you think cats are the smartest animals on earth," Laura said. "But I doubt that cat could read the school rule book. Come on, Steph. Ben will be waiting for you. You know him. If you're ten minutes late, he'll figure you've been kidnapped."

Ben loved a good mystery. He told Stephanie that the main reason he had chosen Chilleen was that he heard the place was haunted. Ben was carrying on a one-man search to find out if it was really true. So far, he'd been unsuccessful.

"And what about you, kitty? Are you a ghost?" Stephanie asked playfully.

The cat's eyes widened at this, then she began to purr.

"Oh, you've started to talk, have you?" Stephanie

crept closer to the kitten. "Come here, pussycat, and tell me who you are. Tell me all about yourself. I'll bet you have a wonderful story."

As she leaned in toward the cat, the green stone charm around her neck began to swing back and forth in the air. The cat followed it with her eyes as if hypnotized.

"You like this?" Stephanie held the necklace out toward the kitten. "Come out and get it, okay, girl?"

Using the charm as bait, Stephanie swung it as she backed slowly away from the bush.

The cat inched out from the bushes and slinked toward Stephanie, her eyes on the charm.

"That's a good kitty. See? I knew we could be friends," Stephanie said. She put out her hand, palm down. The cat came up and rubbed her head beneath it. Then she started to purr louder.

"Aren't you the prettiest thing!" Stephanie gathered the kitten to her and stroked its silky black coat. She rose to her feet with the cat in her arms.

"You know," Stephanie said to Laura, "at first glance, I could have sworn she was a kitten. But now that I'm holding her, I'm beginning to think she's a full-grown cat. Just very small boned and delicate, eh pussums?"

"Sorry, Steph, but she gives me the creeps," Laura said, keeping her distance. She didn't share her friend's love of cats.

"You can't help it if you're not a cat person," Stephanie said. Then she said to the cat, "Can she, girl? Tell me who you are, girl? Are you lost? Are you visiting? Did you stray onto campus from town?"

"Steph, it doesn't really matter if she strayed onto campus from another planet, we've got to go," Laura said, sounding nervous.

Stephanie rubbed the cat under the chin. The animal answered by stretching out her neck and purring happily. Her eyes glowed up at Stephanie.

Stephanie smiled. "I know what it is!" She broke away from the cat's stare. "I know what it is that's odd about her. It's her eyes.

"She's got one green eye . . . and one blue. I don't think I've ever seen that before. I'll have to ask my dad . . ." she trailed off.

The cat was purring steadily now. She was playing, too. She had grabbed the charm between her paws and was batting it about like a catnip mouse.

"So you want to play, huh?" Stephanie said.

The cat tugged on the chain. Stephanie pulled it back in a little game of tug-of-war. Then she saw that the cat's claws had gotten stuck in the fine gold links of her necklace.

"Hold on, kitty," Stephanie said gently. "I'll help free you."

It was too late, though. The creature had started to panic. Like a wild cat caught in a hunter's trap, she began to snarl and thrash about trying to free herself.

The more the cat thrashed, the tighter the chain was pulled around Stephanie's throat. Finally the cat freed one paw. She raised her claws above Stephanie's head. In a second she would slash her face!

CHAPTER 3

"**L**AURA!" Stephanie gasped, ducking back. "Help!"

"I can't get near her!" Laura said helplessly. Finally the cat managed to pull her other paw free. Stephanie held the struggling creature out and away from her so she wouldn't get tangled again.

The cat pawed the air and let out a high-pitched yowl. Then with one swipe of its paw, it scratched Stephanie hard across her hand, leapt into the bushes, and disappeared.

Shocked, Stephanie stood on the path and stared down at the palm of her left hand. She had been scratched by cats plenty of times at the animal hospital. Something about this seemed different, though. Stephanie felt attacked.

"Steph," Laura said in a shaken voice. "Are you okay?"

Stephanie continued to stare at her hand. It hurt, and felt hot.

"You're bleeding!" Laura cried. She untied the scarf from around her braid and handed it to Stephanie. "Sorry I wasn't a bigger help."

"That's okay," Stephanie said faintly. She wrapped the scarf around her hand. She couldn't believe how deep the scratches were.

"Come on," Laura said, taking her arm gently. "Let's get you back to the nurse's office to make sure you don't get an infection. You're really hurt."

"It's nothing. Don't worry about it," Stephanie said. Her hand didn't hurt as much as her feelings. Why had the cat scratched her? She had meant the cat no harm. Probably it was just scared. Homeless and scared and in need of a friend.

As Laura tugged her back along the path toward the nurse's office, Stephanie turned to look at the bushes. Was it her imagination or were those two eyes watching her? At the thought of those strange green and blue eyes, she shivered and walked faster.

They passed the headmistress, Mrs. Danita, on their way to the nurse's. She smiled at them, but her smile faded when she saw their pale faces and the bloodied scarf wrapped around Stephanie's hand.

"What happened?" Mrs. Danita asked, her voice raised in alarm.

"It was this c—" Laura started to say, but Stephanie cut her off.

"It was a cactus," Stephanie said quickly. "I have this plant in my room. I was going to water it, and I tripped and fell into the prickles."

"Goodness!" exclaimed Mrs. Danita. "Next time try to be more careful. Hurry along to the nurse's office and let Mrs. Albert bandage it up for you. It looks nasty. Cactus, you say?" She eyed Stephanie closely.

Stephanie nodded, blushing because of her little fib. She felt uncomfortable about it, and didn't want to get the cat in trouble. "Oh, by the way, Mrs. Danita, you haven't seen a black cat anywhere around here?"

Mrs. Danita paused to think. "Can't say that I have. Old One-Eyed Tom, the stable mouser, is sort of a dirty white color, isn't he?"

Stephanie bit her lip and nodded.

Mrs. Danita continued, "And then there's cook's cat, but she isn't black, either. Other than those two, there are no cats allowed on campus. There are wild cats in the woods, of course, but . . . Why do you ask, Stephanie?"

"Oh, no reason," Stephanie said, trying to sound casual. "I thought I saw one a few minutes ago. But it must have been a shadow."

Mrs. Danita nodded. "I'm sure it was. Because believe me," she added, "I am very allergic to cats. If there's one within fifty feet of me, I start sneezing."

"Well, uh, thanks, Mrs. Danita." Stephanie backed away, smiling politely.

The girls continued on their way to the nurse's office. When they heard Mrs. Danita go into a sneezing fit, they burst out laughing.

"Why did you lie about your hand?" Laura asked through her giggles.

Stephanie frowned. "I guess I just didn't want to get the cat in trouble. I was afraid Mrs. Danita would call in the Animal Protection League or something."

"Which wouldn't be such a bad idea," Laura said. "That's one cat who belongs in kitty jail if you ask me."

"She didn't mean it, Laura."

Laura snorted in disbelief.

"She didn't!" Stephanie insisted. "She was frightened. She didn't know what she was doing. She was just defending herself."

"Give me a break," Laura said. "That's one mean black cat."

At the nurse's office, Mrs. Albert bathed and cleaned Stephanie's wound, then bandaged it.

"I think," she said after she had heard Stephanie's story, "that this cactus of yours had claws. Claws like a cat," she added, eyeing Stephanie closely.

Fifteen minutes later Stephanie met Ben Smith outside the stable. He was sitting on a bale of hay reading his math book. He was so interested in the book, he hadn't heard her.

As Stephanie got closer, she saw why. Inside his math book he had hidden a smaller paperback copy of *The Adventures of Sherlock Holmes*.

"Enjoying your *math?*" Stephanie stood over him, grinning.

Ben slammed both books shut, then grinned back at his friend. His eyes widened when he saw the bandage on her hand.

"Steph, what happened? Is that why you're late?" he asked.

"It's no big deal. Have you looked in on Beulah?"

Ben nodded and followed Stephanie inside the stable to the mare's stall. "She's doing great. Whatever you did, it worked."

Stephanie poked her head over the door of Beulah's stall. She was munching oats peacefully and seemed to be putting weight on her hoof again. Satisfied that Beulah was better, Stephanie and Ben headed back outside. They sat down, back to back, on the bale of hay.

"Might as well start with the first unit," Stephanie said, glumly opening her book.

Ben didn't open his, though. "Let's start with what happened to your hand," he said.

She sighed and turned around to look at him. His unruly light brown hair, long, sharp nose, and dark brown questioning eyes made him look like a pint-size Sherlock Holmes—with braces. Stephanie knew him only too well. He wasn't going to let up until he had a complete report.

"A cat scratched me," she said simply.

"A *cat?* Scratched *you?* What cat?"

He set down his book and reached into his backpack. After taking out a small notebook, he flipped it open to a blank page. Licking the tip of his pencil, he said, "Go on."

Stephanie sighed. She knew there was no stopping Ben once he went into his detective mode. "Well," she began, "she was a stray. I've never seen her before. And she was black. You might as well put your notebook away, because there's really no big mystery."

He copied what she said carefully into the notebook. "A black cat no one's ever seen before scratches you, and you say there's no mystery?" he said.

"The cat kind of pounced on my necklace and got tangled in the chain," Stephanie went on. She held up the charm.

Ben's eyes widened. "Hey! I never saw that before!"

"My mom surprised me with a visit today, just before lunch. She brought this back from Egypt."

Ben pulled out his magnifying glass and examined the necklace.

"Your mom gave this to you? Very interesting. These are hieroglyphs."

"Brilliant deduction, Sherlock."

"I remember there was a famous case involving them." He squinted as he recalled the details. "I believe the detective discovered a mistake in some hieroglyphs on an object in a museum exhibit. The Case of the Egyptian Switch. It seems that the head of this museum was making phony copies of priceless Egyptian stuff. Then he'd sell the real pieces and keep the money." He turned back to Stephanie. "And you say the cat attacked the charm?

"Did your mom tell you what the symbols on it meant?" Ben wanted to know.

Stephanie shook her head.

"Very interesting!" He turned to a fresh page in the notebook and said, "Let's get back to this cat. What did it look like?"

Stephanie smirked. "Like I said, it was a black cat, so it was—*black*."

He grinned, and his braces caught the light. "Any *other* identifying characteristics? Like, did it walk with a limp? Purr with an accent? Wear a patch on its eye?"

Stephanie giggled. "Well, it was full grown, but very small."

"And . . ." Ben prodded.

Stephanie grew serious as she remembered the way the cat had stared at her. "There *was* something else, as a matter of fact," she added.

"Tell me."

"Her eyes. She had one green eye and one blue one."

Ben jumped up so fast, his notebook, pencil, and magnifying glass went flying. "You're kidding!" he cried.

"Of course I'm not kidding. Why should I kid about a thing like that?" Stephanie stared at Ben. His eyes were shining. His cheeks were flushed. She had never seen him this excited.

"You're one hundred percent sure this cat had one green eye and one blue eye?" he asked.

Stephanie nodded.

He picked up his notebook and pencil and began writing quickly. When he finally raised his head, he said, "Okay, Steph, you've got to promise me that the next time you see this animal, no matter where, no matter when, you'll come get me."

"Well," she said, "if it's that important to you."

"It's *very* important," he said. "And there's something else you've got to promise me. You've got to promise—no, swear—that you won't touch that cat again or let it come anywhere near you."

"Sure, but—"

"Because the cat might be dangerous. In fact, Stephanie, it might even be . . . evil."

Stephanie stared at him in disbelief. She felt a sudden pain around her neck and realized that she was pulling on the charm and necklace. She was clutching it as if it had the power . . . to protect her from evil.

CHAPTER 4

"WHAT'S so dangerous about a cat with different-colored eyes?" Laura asked Ben. She set her dinner tray down between Ben and Stephanie at their usual table in the dining room.

She and Stephanie had just gone through the food line. As they chose their dinner, Stephanie filled in Laura on all the questions Ben had asked at the stable.

Ben was shoveling mashed potatoes and sausage into his mouth as if he were trying to win a food race.

"I've asked Ben the same question about a hundred times," Stephanie said, "but he's not telling why he's so worried about me and the cat."

Laura seemed to be disappointed. "Come on, Ben. Share. You know what they tell first graders: sharing's the way to have fun."

"I will share," Ben said, wiping his milk mustache

off with a paper napkin, "when I feel the time is right. In the meantime . . ." He took out his notebook. "Very quickly now, because I have to leave in a minute, I'd like to hear your version of what happened with the cat this afternoon, Laura." He licked the point of his pencil and stared at her.

"Well," Laura began eagerly, "that cat sure was creepy."

"You can't go by that," Stephanie said with a laugh. "Laura thinks all cats are creepy."

"True," Laura admitted, "but this one was creepier. Maybe it was the eyes."

"Mind if I join you?" said a girl's voice.

It was Jane Trent. She lived across the hall from Stephanie and Laura.

"Sure," Ben said. He shoved his notebook into his pocket. "We were just talking about the chess tournament, weren't we, girls?" He stared meaningfully at them.

Stephanie nodded to show she understood his message—*Don't mention the cat.*

Laura nodded, too. She started talking about the stories for that week's school newspaper. Both Laura and Jane were reporters for the *Chilleen Canyon Echo.*

"I'd rather report on the chess tournament than the art show," Laura said to Jane. "You're good in art, so you cover the art show."

"That's right!" Ben broke in. "You're taking art class this semester, aren't you, Jane?"

Jane nodded. "It's my favorite subject."

"Great!" Ben said. "You don't have any art supplies with you, by any chance? Like a stick of charcoal, maybe? Or even a crayon?"

"Let me see." Jane pulled her oversize purse off the back of her chair and rummaged around in it. "I've got some charcoal. Do you want one stick or two?" she asked.

"Two, just in case one breaks."

"Why do you need charcoal?" Stephanie asked. Ben was up to something, she could tell. He had that look.

"Oh, nothing. A simple science experiment, that's all," he said. "And can I have your extra paper napkin, Jane?"

Jane shrugged. "Help yourself."

"Thanks." Ben smiled. He wrapped the charcoal sticks carefully in the napkin and tucked them in the back pocket of his jeans.

"Well, guys," Ben said, standing up and lifting his dinner tray. "Sorry to run off like this, but I've got a ton of homework. See you tomorrow at breakfast."

"Now, what do you suppose he's up to?" Laura wondered out loud as the three of them watched Ben drop off his tray and jog out of the dining room.

"I don't know, but I'm going to find out," Stephanie said, pushing back her chair and following after Ben.

Where in the world did Ben think he was going? Stephanie wondered as she followed about thirty feet behind him. He wasn't going to his room to do his homework, that was for sure. He was cutting across the lawn toward the woods. It was obvious he didn't expect to be followed, because he never once glanced behind him. Stephanie was glad of that.

Ben took a narrow, rarely used path into the woods. Stephanie stayed about thirty paces behind him. She heard his sneakers crunching twigs up ahead.

Why was he going into the woods just as the sun was setting? It wasn't her idea of fun. The trees on either side of the path blocked out what little light there was. She felt a shiver run down her spine in the gloomy darkness. Ben took a left where the path forked. Suddenly Stephanie knew exactly where he was going.

To the Chilleen family graveyard!

She stopped and swallowed, her heart pounding in her chest. Did she really want to follow him there?

A bunch of kids had gone there last Halloween for fun. The fun had turned pretty scary when some older kids swooped down on them. They had been draped in white sheets. The younger kids had been so frightened, they screamed all the way back to campus and had nightmares for days.

Stephanie shook off her fear and went on. There would be no kids dressed up like ghosts now, she told herself. Besides, she needed to find out what

Ben was up to. What did he know that he wasn't telling her?

Up ahead, Ben was already at the graveyard. She stopped on the edge of the cemetery, and hid behind a bushy pine.

The graveyard was quite large, but Stephanie wasn't surprised about that. The Chilleens were once the biggest, most powerful family in the valley. Stephanie tried to imagine the graveyard as it must have looked years ago: the grass mowed, the sparkling marble tombstones standing in neat rows, fresh flowers at every grave.

Now the cemetery was full of weeds and poorly tended. Some of the grave markers had even toppled over. In the fading light, they threw twisted shadows here and there.

None of this seemed to bother Ben as he waded through the weeds. She watched as he stopped at a small grave. He looked down at it for a few minutes. She saw his lips moving. Was he talking to himself or to the person in the grave? she wondered. Then he moved two rows over and a little to the left, to another, larger gravestone.

Stephanie saw a flash of something white. It was the paper dinner napkin! Ben bent over the tombstone. He was doing something with the napkin—but what?

Whatever it was, Stephanie wished he'd hurry up. Around her, the woods became blacker and scarier with every passing second.

Overhead, she heard an eerie hoot and jumped.

It's only an owl, Stephanie, she told herself. *And that sound like werewolves howling in the hills? It is probably only coyotes. Unless it really is werewolves. Don't be silly, Stephanie,* she said, and hugged herself. *There's no such thing as werewolves, or ghosts, or evil cats, either.*

Ben seemed perfectly at ease, even pleased with himself. He rose, folded the napkin, and made his way back across the graveyard.

Stephanie waited until he'd disappeared a ways down the path. Ignoring her fear, she crept out from behind the tree and made her way through the weeds into the graveyard. She stumbled on a fallen tombstone, but managed to catch her balance.

Finally she reached the smaller of the two graves Ben had visited. A small bouquet of dried flowers lay at its base. She peered at the words engraved on it, but it was too dark to make them out now.

She sighed and shivered. She'd have to come back the next day to check out the other grave and conduct a full investigation, as Ben would say.

Having decided that, Stephanie ran back to campus as fast as she could.

Laura and Stephanie lay on their beds later that night, studying. Stephanie had decided not to tell Laura about following Ben. She knew Laura spooked easily, and didn't want to upset her.

It was a warm spring evening, and Stephanie had cracked the window near her bed. The room was filled with the fresh smell of pine needles.

She read about Greek history until lights-out. Then she and Laura switched off their reading lamps and wished each other sweet dreams.

Stephanie fell asleep that night, as on so many other nights, staring up into the glow-in-the-dark eyes of the Persian cat in the poster on her ceiling. As she drifted off to sleep she seemed to hear the cat purr. . . .

It wasn't the Persian cat, though, it was the black cat! She stood outside the window, staring in at Stephanie with those eerie eyes. Then she squeezed in under the partially open window and jumped down onto the chair next to the bed.

Overjoyed to see her again, Stephanie reached out to stroke the cat. Before her very eyes, the cat grew bigger. It was taking on a human shape—the shape of a woman!

She was a beautiful woman. Long, silky coal black hair fell down her shoulders. She wore a gown of red silk, with threads of gold and silver. Her nails were clawlike. She turned and looked at Stephanie. Her eyes—one green, one blue—seemed to burn into Stephanie's very soul.

She opened her blood-red lips and began to speak. Stephanie tried to understand it, but it was a language she had never heard. It was full of harsh sounds. A language from some distant time and place.

Then Stephanie noticed that the smell of pine needles was gone. The air in the room now smelled of strange and exotic spices. Someone was burning incense!

The woman leaned forward in the chair as she spoke faster and faster. Her hand gestures grew wilder and more frantic, the long nails flashing like tiny daggers. Finally she burst into tears, the teardrops flowing down her lovely smooth cheeks.

Then, without warning, the woman lunged forward and grabbed Stephanie's necklace. The woman wrapped her hands tightly around the chain, and pulled Stephanie closer to her.

The woman's face was now so close to Stephanie's that Stephanie could feel the moist heat of her breath. The words were whispered harshly. And at last, one word separated itself from the babble. One word that Stephanie could understand. That word was *Return!*

Every time the woman said, "Return," she wound the necklace chain tighter. She was cutting off Stephanie's supply of air! Stephanie's eyes bulged. Her mouth opened wide in a silent scream as she fought for breath—for life.

Stephanie woke from her strange dream, her heart pounding. Laura was already gone. The morning light streaming through the curtains seemed unreal compared to the dream. She closed her eyes again, trying to calm herself.

Then she felt it. There was a warm weight pressing down on her chest. Her throat was burning. Stephanie opened her eyes and realized that what was happening was no dream! The black cat had gotten into her room and was sitting on her chest. The cat's paws were clawing at the chain around her neck. The cat was trying to choke the life out of her!

CHAPTER 5

STEPHANIE quickly felt for the cat's front paws. One by one, she lifted the sharp claws from the links of the chain. She sucked in a big gulp of air before lifting the cat off her chest and setting her down at the foot of the bed.

Stephanie moved away from the cat and leaned against the headboard. She eyed the cat warily as she rubbed her sore neck.

The cat stood up and stared at her, shivering from head to tail, as if someone had just dunked her in ice-cold water.

Even though the cat had nearly strangled her, Stephanie felt her heart begin to melt. "Come here, kitty. I forgive you," she said.

Then, when Stephanie reached out to touch her, the cat arched her back and hissed. Suddenly the promise she had made to Ben came back. She was to tell him the next time she saw the cat, no matter when, no matter where—and not to touch it.

Stephanie got up slowly and closed the window. She'd shut the cat up in the room while she ran to get Ben. He was probably already down in the dining room at breakfast.

The cat followed her as Stephanie edged toward the door.

"Why don't you settle down on the bed and take a nap? I'll be back in just a minute. Okay, kitty?" The cat growled deep in her throat and leapt—no, *flew*—over Stephanie's head. She landed on top of the wardrobe. The wardrobe was at least six feet off the floor!

Stephanie stared up at her, openmouthed. Just then Laura, in bathrobe and slippers, swung open the door. "Hey, Steph—" she started to say.

The cat leapt down off her perch. She streaked toward Laura, who let out a sudden shrill scream.

"Return!" hissed the cat as she raced out the door.

"Does that cat have wings?" Laura cried.

Stephanie didn't answer. *Forget about wings! That cat just spoke.* And he said the same word Stephanie had heard in her dream: *Return!*

Stephanie sped out the door after the cat.

"Let it go!" Laura called after her.

"I can't!"

The cat raced down the hall, Stephanie right after her. The animal dived through the swinging door to the bathroom, Stephanie following. "Here, kitty! Kitty!"

The bathroom was really crowded. Everyone was showering and getting ready. The air was thick with steam and girls' chatter.

"Here, kitty, kitty!" Stephanie peered through the mist. She looked beneath the stalls, behind the robes and towels hanging on hooks along the wall, but saw no sign of the cat.

"Anybody see a cat run in here?" Stephanie's voice, bouncing off the tiles, sounded strange to her ears.

The chatter stopped. Then one girl ran out of a shower stall, a towel draped around her, her hair sudsy with shampoo. "Eek! A black rat!" she shrieked.

Other girls joined in the panic. "Rat!" they screamed. "A black rat in the girls' bathroom!"

A panicked group of girls ran out the door. Stephanie saw a black blur follow at their heels. It was the cat!

Stephanie followed her down the hall. The cat dashed down the staircase toward the front door. Stephanie couldn't let her get away.

"Here, kitty, kitty."

A couple of girls were coming up the stairs on their way back from the dining room. They stared as Stephanie pounded barefoot down past them.

"Kitty! Kitty! Here, kitty, kitty!" she shouted. She burst into the study room off to her left and looked frantically around. She checked under every chair, even up the chimney! No sign of the cat. Stephanie bit her lip. What if one of the teachers caught her searching for a cat? She'd be in trouble. So would the cat. She had to find that cat.

Then she saw the tip of a black tail as it slipped out the door. "There you are. Kitty, kitty!" she exclaimed.

Stephanie followed her out into the main hall and then into the dayroom.

She stood in the doorway and looked around. A bunch of kids were sitting around drinking cocoa and watching cartoons on television.

They all stopped to watch Stephanie instead.

"Anyone here see where that black kitty went?" she asked, out of breath.

A boy burst out laughing and said, "What happened to you, Steph? Did you lose your itty-bitty kitty cat?"

"Care for a bowl of cocoa, kitty?" another boy asked.

She tried to ignore them as she continued her search. She pulled back drapes, lifted the couch cushions, peered behind the furniture, calling, "Here, kitty, kitty!"

By now a bunch of other kids had come to stand in the doorway and watch. *Don't they have anything better to do?* Stephanie wondered.

"Hey, Steph, since when have they changed the dress code around here?" someone called.

Stephanie froze. The "here, kitty, kitty" died on her lips. She realized what all the fuss was about. She was standing in the dayroom in broad daylight wearing nothing but a shortie nightshirt!

She glanced down at herself. The hot pink night-shirt had a babyish furry kitty sewn on it. Underneath the picture, in letters made up of glitter and sequins, were the words "Cuddly Kitten."

Her mother had sent the shirt to her from Japan. It was her favorite nightie. She felt herself blushing. She smiled uneasily, tugging the hem down over her bare knees.

"You look almost as cute as my baby sister does in her little nightgown," called out another kid.

By now Stephanie was bright red. *Forget about the cat*, she told herself. She yanked a blanket off a chair and covered herself with it. Without a word, she stomped up the stairs to her room.

That cat, she fumed, *isn't evil. It's just a big pain!*

CHAPTER 6

BY the time Stephanie had come back downstairs after showering and dressing for the day, just about everybody had heard about the Cuddly Kitten Episode.

Stephanie wasn't surprised about that. The Chilleen campus was like a small town. Word had spread that Stephanie Markson had been seen that morning streaking around in her kitty nightie.

Kids were saying that cat-lover Stephanie Markson had finally gone totally nuts. She was seeing cats everywhere. Big, pink, furry kitty cats with sequins for eyes and collars made of glitter.

"Well, if it isn't the Cuddly Kitten herself!" Bobby Worth teased her on the way down to breakfast.

"Meow," she heard some kids saying behind her in the breakfast line. "What's for breakfast, Kitty Kibbles?"

Stephanie gritted her teeth as she set her tray down next to Laura. She considered herself a good sport normally, but this was really starting to get to her.

"Just ignore them," Laura said. "They're a bunch of jerks."

"You saw the cat, didn't you?" Stephanie asked. "You know I didn't imagine it."

"Of course I saw the cat!" Laura said.

Stephanie leaned in close and whispered, "Laura, that cat *talked* to me this morning!"

Laura looked doubtful. "Wait a minute. You say this cat talked to you? Like . . . in English?"

Stephanie nodded. "She said, 'Return.' "

" 'Return'," Laura repeated, seeming really confused. "Tell Ben about it. I'm sure he'll be thrilled to have a new clue. First he had a cat with two different-colored eyes. Then he had an *evil* cat with two different-colored eyes. Now he has a *talking* evil cat with two different-colored eyes. Only thing I can't figure out is, why would a cat say *return?*"

Stephanie heaved her shoulders. "How should I know? Maybe she's lost and wants to be returned to her master."

Laura nodded. "Could be as simple as that. Ben would be pretty disappointed."

"Well, he won't be after he hears about the dream I had last night," answered Stephanie.

"What dream?" Laura asked, pushing her glasses

up on her nose. "Tell me about it. Oh, yikes!" she said, glancing at the wall clock. "I've got music in five minutes, Steph. I've got to run. Tell me your dream later."

All morning long Stephanie was on the lookout for the little black cat. She felt sure that the cat was nearby, darting through the bushes, peering out at her from behind doors, mewing.

In English, Stephanie was sitting at her desk, reading a poem with the rest of the class. Then she felt those eyes boring into the top of her skull. She jerked her head up. The black cat was standing outside her window. Her tail was twitching, and her eyes were burning into Stephanie.

"Wait for me, kitty," she whispered. "Wait till after class."

"Well, Stephanie?" Mrs. Filmore was saying.

Stephanie looked away from the window. "Yes, Mrs. Filmore?"

The teacher smiled. "Stephanie Markson, I've asked you the same question three times. What is the poem we are reading about?"

Stephanie stammered, "Um, well, it's about, um . . ."

"Maybe it's about a kitty cat," the boy next to her whispered with a chuckle.

"Well, Stephanie?" Mrs. Filmore asked again.

Stephanie stared at the teacher with her mouth open.

"What's the matter, Stephanie?" Mrs. Filmore said gently. "You don't seem yourself today."

"Cat got your tongue?" a boy in the back of the room called out.

The class burst into laughter.

Stephanie's cheeks burned with embarrassment. She stared over at the window, but the cat was gone. She stared back at her desk, at her shaking hands holding her book.

"All right, settle down, class," Mrs. Filmore said.

Stephanie wished she were a million miles away. She tried to concentrate on the poem in the book, but she couldn't stop her hands from trembling.

It was then that she noticed them.

Her fingernails.

She had always had ugly fingernails. Ugly because they refused to grow very long. They always split or broke off before she could grow them long enough to shape them.

Now her nails were long, twice as long as they had ever been.

This was too strange!

As soon as English class ended, Stephanie raced back to her room, hoping to find Laura. She needed to show Laura her nails. Only yesterday morning she had been complaining to her friend about how short and stumpy her nails were. Laura had told her that she needed to drink more milk. The minerals in milk would make her nails grow, she'd said. Could one extra glass of milk make nails grow this quickly? She had to find out.

Laura wasn't there, though. She couldn't ask Ben, because he was at a special session with his history teacher, Mrs. Douglas. They were planning his term paper, on his favorite subject, mysteries. It was called "The Great Mysteries of History."

Stephanie had a free period before her next class, and she knew exactly how to spend it. She bounded down the main staircase and out onto the front porch, where she checked her watch. She had exactly forty minutes. Enough time for a quick visit to the Chilleen family graveyard.

When Stephanie got to the tombstone with the dried flowers, she stopped. They were held together with a rubber band, and didn't look as if they'd come from a store. They were asters and daisies. Stephanie realized they were the same flowers that sometimes stood in the little vases on the school's dining room tables.

She set down the flowers and read the writing on the small, crude tombstone aloud:

"Noah Farnsworth 1886 to 1929. Manservant to Ambrose Chilleen. May God rest his soul."

"Ambrose Chilleen." She repeated the name as she went to find his grave. She read the names on the markers as she wound her way up one of the rows of tombstones and down the other. They were all Chilleens, by birth or by marriage: Ebeneezer, Aldrich, Raymond, Cuthbert, Morgana, Prudence, Ambey, Allegra. Two rows over and slightly to the left, she found the grave of Ambrose Chilleen. Just as she'd suspected, it was the same grave that Ben had visited the night before.

It had the biggest marker in the yard. It was a bronze statue of a man standing on a slab of black marble. He wore high boots and riding pants, a jacket full of pockets, and a helmet. He looked like an old-time explorer. He had a mustache and a sharp, pointed beard.

Stephanie squinted up at him. She liked the outfit, but she didn't care much for the face. He looked kind of mean.

She lowered her gaze back to the marble slab and the words on it: Tragically fallen in his youth.

Interesting, Stephanie thought. Ambrose had died in 1929, the same year as his servant, Noah Farnsworth. She wondered if there was a connection.

Then she noticed something else.

At the base of the marble slab was a smaller stone. It was lighter in color than the marble. Carved into this stone was a symbol that looked like an Egyptian hieroglyph!

After school Stephanie went to the stables, looking for Ben. Vernon, the man in charge of the horses, was in the stable. He was brushing a big bay.

Stephanie stroked the horse's strong neck.

"Ben went out riding," Vernon said. "He told me he was going up by Clover Meadow."

"I think I'll saddle up Rusty and join him," she said.

"Suit yourself, Stephie. You're Rusty's favorite rider," Vernon said.

She saddled up Rusty and mounted him, hoping Ben hadn't changed his mind and gone riding somewhere else. She had to talk to him. Maybe he could help her figure out what was going on.

Rusty knew the way from the stable up the path to the meadow. Stephanie just sat and let Rusty do the work.

As she rode, she fiddled with the necklace around her neck. Now she knew something that she hadn't known before. Her charm and Ambrose Chilleen's gravestone had something in common—hieroglyphs. Was it just a coincidence? She felt sure that Ben would know the answer.

The pine trees were beginning to thin out. The afternoon rays of the sun shone down on her. Clover Meadow was just ahead. Eagerly Rusty started to trot toward it. Stephanie looked ahead at the meadow, but saw no sign of Ben. As they broke into the open, Stephanie urged Rusty into a canter.

Suddenly Rusty let out a frightened whinny. Stephanie felt his muscles stiffen beneath her. He was about to rear! She had just enough time to pull her boots out of the stirrups before he reared into the air and threw her.

Stephanie sailed backward through the air and landed with a crash in the weeds.

She tried to lift her head, but it felt too heavy. Then everything went black.

CHAPTER 7

*T*HE smell of incense filled Stephanie's nostrils. The air was rich and heavy with it as Stephanie's eyes opened to the sight of the cat woman. Her long black hair and ankle-length red gown were blowing in the breeze. Stephanie realized that the woman must have scared Rusty.

The cat woman opened blood-red lips and began to speak. As before, the odd, harsh words were totally foreign to Stephanie. Then she heard the one word she could understand: *Return!*

But return where? Return what? Stephanie didn't understand. The woman hissed and pulled Stephanie roughly to her feet.

Stephanie stumbled after the woman across the meadow—but it wasn't a meadow anymore! *What had happened to Clover Meadow?*

Instead of weeds and wildflowers, there were tall grasses. In place of the pines, there were palm and date trees full of fruit. And the air! The air was no longer dry and smelling of pine and clover. It smelled of damp grass and mud and river water!

The woman parted a curtain of tall grass. Stephanie saw a river, wide and powerful and muddy, in the opening.

A boat glided past. It was long and graceful, its golden hull carved in the shape of a crocodile.

Stephanie turned away from the river. Behind them, over the tops of the palms, a palace rose. Its tall pillars gleamed in the hot sun.

Then she heard a voice, a girl's voice, calling out to her right.

The cat woman dropped Stephanie's hand and ran eagerly toward the sound of the voice. Before Stephanie's eyes, the cat woman turned into the little black cat. She leapt up into the arms of the young girl.

The girl was about Stephanie's age. Her skin was a coppery color, and her shiny black hair was done in dozens of small braids, each tipped with a golden bead. She wore golden sandals and a long, stiff golden skirt with a halter top. Around her neck she wore a single, simple piece of jewelry. With a shock, Stephanie realized that it was identical to the necklace hanging around her own neck!

The girl and the cat sat down on a stone bench. The girl stroked the cat and said, "Don't you know you're my only friend in the world? Especially now that my beloved father, the king, is dead."

Suddenly a man approached from the palace. His head was completely bald and gleaming with oils. His eyes were black, and he was frowning.

"So here you are!" he said gruffly.

"Uncle!" the girl cried. She clutched the cat more tightly to her chest.

"You will never grow up to be Queen of the Nile if you spend all your time in the garden with this foolish cat. It is time for your birthday feast."

The cat arched its back and hissed at the uncle. The princess drew herself up tall and said, "I don't *want* a birthday feast. Send the guests away!"

"What foolishness!" the uncle said. He clapped his big hands. Two large men appeared and grabbed the girl. The uncle snatched the cat from her arms.

"Give her back to me!" she cried, struggling to free herself.

The men ignored her as they carried her off to the palace.

"As for you!" the uncle said to the cat. "I've had enough of you!"

His huge hands tightened around the cat's throat.

Stephanie screamed, "Leave her alone!"

CHAPTER 8

STEPHANIE struggled to sit up. "The princess! I have to help her! She's in danger!" she shouted.

"Steph, it's me, Ben. Are you okay? What princess?"

Stephanie's eyes opened and came to rest on Ben. He was kneeling over her, looking worried.

"Ben?" she whispered.

Relief passed over his face. He pulled off his riding helmet and wiped the sweat from his forehead. "You had me worried," he said.

"How did you get here?" she asked. "Where's the evil uncle? Where's the black cat?"

Ben seemed worried again.

Stephanie tried to explain. "It's the princess who owns the black cat. Her uncle came and made her go to her birthday party. . . . Her life's in danger, I know it! I have to . . ." Stephanie's speech trailed off as she glanced around. "Where are the palm trees? Where's the palace?" she asked.

Ben whistled softly. "That must have been some knock on the head."

"But you don't understand . . ." Stephanie shook her head. She took off her riding helmet and felt her head. She seemed to be in one piece, even if her thoughts were crazy. "Nothing. Never mind," she said, certain Ben would never believe what had just happened to her.

She started to get up but felt a little dizzy. Ben helped her sit back down and said, "I'll tie your horse up here and let it graze. I'll come back for it later. Right now we'll ride double and take you to the nurse."

Ben helped a shaky Stephanie into the nurse's office. While Mrs. Albert checked her out, Ben took care of the horses.

Stephanie spent the next few hours lying on a cot. Mrs. Albert kept a cold washcloth on Stephanie's forehead to ease the pain.

That evening Laura and Jane went to visit Stephanie.

"We're debating whether or not to make you the subject of this week's lead story," Laura said. "Expert Horsewoman Gets Tossed. How's it sound as a headline?"

"Don't you dare," said Stephanie. She took off the

washcloth and sat up. At least she wasn't dizzy anymore.

"You okay?" Laura asked.

Stephanie nodded. She wanted to tell Laura about the dream, but not while Jane was there.

They sat around talking about classes and friends. Finally Jane glanced at her watch. "I've got to run. See you two later. Feel better, Steph!" she said.

She picked up her backpack and left. Except for Mrs. Albert, who was typing forms in her small office, Stephanie and Laura were the only ones in the infirmary.

"You look terrible," Laura said.

"Thanks," Stephanie said sarcastically.

"I mean . . . you look like you saw a ghost," Laura said. Her voice echoed eerily in the large room.

"I'm beginning to think I did. I had another dream," Stephanie said.

Laura pulled nervously on her braid. "You want to tell me?"

"Yeah, but first . . . take a look at these."

Stephanie held up her hands and showed off her new long fingernails.

"Yikes, Steph!" Laura exclaimed. "Fake nails? I know you want to grow them long, but I didn't think you were the type to buy fake ones."

"I'm *not* the type," Stephanie said impatiently. "And these aren't fake. These are real. Since this morning."

Laura stared at the ten daggerlike fingernails. "This isn't funny anymore, Steph. What's going on? I mean it!"

"These dreams . . ." Stephanie said.

Laura pulled her chair in closer. "Talk," she said.

Stephanie told Laura everything, about her dream the night before when the cat turned into a cat woman. And about the dream in the meadow, with the princess and the evil uncle.

Laura listened in silence, her eyes growing rounder, her freckles dark against her pale face.

When Stephanie finished, Laura shivered and looked as if she wanted to crawl under the covers with her friend. Stephanie knew exactly how she felt. Suddenly the room seemed too big. There were too many windows. Too many windows through which unknown eyes might be peering in at them right then.

"What's going on, Steph?" Laura whispered. "What's *happening* to you?"

"I don't know. But I've got a feeling Ben knows something that he isn't telling. You know what I think? I think he's finally found a real true mystery, and he wants to keep it all to himself. Well, he's—"

"How are you girls doing?" came a voice in the darkened doorway. It was Mrs. Albert. "My, but it's dark in here!" she said. Then she went around turning on switches, flooding the big room with light.

"How's the head, Stephanie? Feel well enough to join the human race again?" she asked.

Stephanie leaned back against the pillow. "Actually, my headache's come back. I think I need another aspirin."

Mrs. Albert felt her pulse, then her head. "I wouldn't be surprised if you're suffering a mild concussion. It was a good thing you were wearing your helmet. Now let's take a look at those cactus scratches while I've got you here," she said.

Stephanie held out her left hand.

Mrs. Albert peeled off the adhesive tape and lifted the bandage.

She nodded and seemed pleased.

"How am I doing?" Stephanie asked.

"Quite nicely. A good scab has formed. I don't think you need to wear a bandage anymore. It would be better to let it air out. Just keep it clean. And wear gloves when you muck out the stables."

Mrs. Albert went to get Stephanie some aspirin, leaving the girls alone again.

"Yikes!" Laura exclaimed. She pointed at Stephanie's hand.

"What?" Stephanie said.

"Look at your hand! Look at the scratches, Steph! Look at them!"

Stephanie stared at the scratches. She blinked, held

her hand closer, and stared again. Then she held her hand and the necklace charm side by side and compared them.

There was no mistaking it.

The scabs on her hand had healed into the exact same pattern as the hieroglyphs on her charm!

CHAPTER 9

STEPHANIE couldn't wait for the next day to be over. Ben had gone on a field trip with his biology class, and she had to wait until evening to show him her hand.

She and Laura met him in the library, on the second floor of the main building. Stephanie showed him her nails first, but he wasn't especially impressed by them. He'd never noticed her fingernails in the first place, he explained.

Then she showed him the scabs on her hand. His eyes widened, and he whipped out a magnifying glass and grabbed her hand. He pulled her over to a reading lamp and examined her palm carefully.

After a while he lowered the glass, his brown eyes sparkling. "This is really incredible!" he said.

"Wait," Laura said. "You haven't heard anything yet. Tell him about the dreams, Steph."

Stephanie quickly told him about the two dreams. By now he seemed ready to burst with excitement. "This is really, truly incredible!" he said.

"We know it's incredible, Ben. But what does it mean?" Stephanie asked.

Ben shook his head. "I don't know. This scab business is strange, but I once read about a case like it. The Case of the Scalding Scarab, they called it. Do you know what a scarab is?"

"Sure," said Laura. "It's a stone carved in the shape of a bug."

Ben continued. "This thief tried to steal one that was in a jewelry shop window. The sun heated the stone, and it was so hot, it burned its pattern on the thief's palm. That's how they caught him in the end."

Ben examined Stephanie's charm beneath the magnifying glass. "I wish we could read these symbols. I wonder if my history teacher, Mrs. Douglas, can read them. We could show her the charm and your hand and see what she makes of it."

Stephanie put her hand deep into the pocket of her flowered miniskirt. "No way! She'll think we're all nuts," she said.

"I know!" Laura spoke up. "Maybe there's a dictionary on this kind of writing here in the library. Maybe we could figure out the symbols ourselves."

"It's worth a try," Ben said. "I'll ask the librarian. Laura, you check the card catalog and get out all the books on Egypt. Maybe we can find out if this princess and her uncle ever existed. Got it?"

"Yeah. Good idea," Laura said.

Ben turned to Stephanie. "You should go downstairs and Xerox your hand."

"Excuse me? *Xerox?* My hand? Stephanie asked.

Ben grinned. "Haven't you ever done that before for a joke? Just stick your hand down on the glass and push the button. We need to have a picture of what your hand looks like now. Who knows? You might wake up tomorrow with the scabs all gone."

"Brilliant idea, Sherlock," Stephanie said, calling Ben Sherlock Holmes, after Ben's hero.

Stephanie went downstairs to use the copy machine on the ground floor near the school office. Luckily she had a lot of change, because it took her several tries to get a clear picture.

A boy waiting for the machine looked at Stephanie as if she were nuts. She grinned at him as if this were just her idea of a great time.

In the end she was happy with the results. The tiny symbols from her hand showed up sharply and clearly.

When she got back upstairs with the copies, she found Laura and Ben sitting at a table behind a huge stack of books. There was no such thing as a dictionary of ancient Egyptian writing, they told her. But there were tons of books about ancient Egypt. Now they were going through each one searching for clues.

"Sit down and grab a book," Ben invited her.

By nine o'clock Stephanie's eyes were burning. Her fingers were gritty with a thin coat of book dust. She had found out lots of facts about ancient Egypt, though.

She learned about the royal courts and their complex ceremonies and many riches. She read of the Egyptians' belief in magic and life after death. To be sure their dead bodies would last forever, the Egyptians had embalmers make them into mummies. The exact way they did it was still a mystery to modern experts.

Bodies were brought to a place called the Beautiful House, where they were turned into mummies.

The tombs for the bodies were huge, like houses. The more powerful the person in life, the grander and larger the tomb. The tombs were especially designed so that robbers couldn't enter them and make off with the riches buried with the dead. Thick doors of stone and false passages were built to keep robbers away. Scary-looking statues of gods were placed at every corner to frighten off robbers and force them to turn back.

"Listen to this," Stephanie said, breaking the silence. "The ancient Egyptians worshiped the cat as a god. Pet cats were often buried in the tombs. They were mummified and placed in tiny coffins."

"Cool!" Ben said.

"Creepy!" Laura said, shivering.

Just then the second of three warning bells went off. It signaled that the library would be closing in five minutes.

Stephanie rose and stretched. So did Ben. Wearily they began to gather up the books.

"Come on, Laura," Ben said, yawning. "The librarian's going to come and kick us out."

But Laura didn't seem to hear him. She was sitting, staring down at the open book before her.

It was a very old book. Its binding was crumbling, and its pages were tissue-thin and yellowed with age.

"Wow!" she exclaimed. She flipped her braid back over her shoulder so that it bounced on her back.

Stephanie stopped stacking books and stared at her friend. "What is it?" she asked.

"This book," Laura explained. "It's written by that guy Clancy."

Stephanie nodded. She had come across Horace Clancy's name several times that evening. Back in the 1920s he had discovered several ancient tombs.

"Horace Clancy, the famous archaeologist. What about him?" Ben said, glancing at his watch.

"Look! Both of you! Look at this picture!" cried Laura.

Stephanie and Ben peered over Laura's shoulder at the picture she was pointing to. It was a faded photograph of a young man in a helmet and riding pants. He was standing beside a small mummy case. He had a mustache and a small, pointy beard.

Stephanie's heart started to race, and her throat suddenly felt dry. She knew where she'd seen that man before. He was the statue. The one in the graveyard.

"So?" Ben said. "That's Clancy, right?"

"Wrong," Stephanie whispered. "I'm sure his name is Chilleen. Ambrose Chilleen."

Ben's face suddenly became very pale. He rubbed his eyes and sat down heavily in the nearest chair. "Okay," he said quietly, "I see the time has come . . . for me to tell you what I know about this case."

CHAPTER 10

"**A**T last!" said Stephanie.

"It's about time," said Laura. "Cough it up."

Both Stephanie and Laura started closing in on Ben. They backed him up against a row of library books.

He laughed uneasily. "Hey, I said I'd share, didn't I? Just give me a chance. I need to tell this the right way. From the beginning."

"A good place to start," Stephanie said.

"Excellent," Laura agreed.

"*Now*, Ben," Stephanie said, crossing her arms.

"Quit stalling. It's getting late," Laura added. "And we don't have all night."

Just then the last warning bell rang and the three of them jumped.

"Haunting the stacks at this late hour?" a voice asked them. It was Ben's history teacher, Mrs. Douglas. Her arms were full of test booklets.

"Ben!" she said. "I'm so glad you're here. Would you mind giving me a hand carrying these test booklets back down to my office?"

Giving the girls an apologetic look, Ben said, "Sure, Mrs. Douglas. I'd be happy to."

Glancing at the books on the table, Mrs. Douglas said approvingly, "Ah, ancient Egypt! Land of the Pharaohs! Land of Mystery! A very fascinating subject."

"You're not kidding," Ben agreed. He took the Xerox of Stephanie's hand, folded it, and stuffed it in his pocket. Then he took half the test booklets and followed Mrs. Douglas downstairs.

Stephanie was standing outside the stable the next morning, waiting for Ben.

"Let's talk," she said as soon as he showed up.

"Let's feed the horses first," he said. "You take the north side, I'll take the south. I'll meet you back here afterward. Vernon said he wants us to soap the saddles and bridles today."

"Oh, all right," Stephanie said. She knew he wasn't going to escape this time.

By the time she got back, Ben was already applying saddle soap to a bridle. He was whistling, as if he hadn't a care in the world.

Stephanie stood in the doorway, hands on her hips.

"All right, Ben. Suppose you start by telling me who Noah Farnsworth is and why you put flowers on his grave."

Ben tossed Stephanie a rag and a tin of soap. "I do it once a year. On April sixteenth, his birthday. It's the least I can do. You see, Noah Farnsworth was my great-grandfather."

"Your great-grandfather!" Stephanie repeated.

"He and his wife came to America from the north of England. They got jobs working for Ambrose Chilleen, who had just moved into this house. Seven members of Ambrose's family had died in a fire in the house, and it had been empty for several years before he bought it and fixed it up. Great-Grandma was the maid. Great-Grandpa was Ambrose Chilleen's personal servant."

"Wow" was all Stephanie could say.

Ben continued, "My great-grandmother is still alive. She remembers Ambrose Chilleen like it was yesterday. Ambrose was a rich man. And, like lots of rich men, he had hobbies to fill up his time. His favorite hobby was archaeology, or the study of the way people lived long ago. He was very interested in Egypt. It was Ambrose Chilleen who gave Clancy the money for that journey to Egypt."

"So *that* was why his picture was in that book. He must have gone on the tour with Clancy," said Stephanie.

Ben nodded. "Clancy probably had no choice but to invite the guy, even though he must have been a real pest.

"It was on this trip," Ben went on, lugging a saddle

across the room and draping it over a sawhorse, "that Clancy made an important discovery of some tombs. Actually, a whole group of tombs. In the upper Nile Valley."

"Did your great-grandfather go along as Ambrose's servant?" Stephanie wanted to know.

Ben shook his head. "For some reason, Noah didn't go with Ambrose to Egypt. All my great-grandmother remembers is that it was good to have Ambrose gone from the estate for a while. He wasn't very nice, you see. She said they were all really disappointed when he came home from his travels early."

"How come?"

"He got sick or something. No one was sure."

Stephanie waited for him to go on, but he didn't. "That's it?" she asked, feeling let down.

He shook his head. "That's just the beginning. It was after the trip that strange things started happening to Ambrose back here in Phantom Valley."

"Like what?"

Ben took a deep breath, then said, "He was working on some mysterious project up in the woods, by the cemetery. No one was allowed up there, so no one knew what he was up to."

"And?" Stephanie urged him on.

"And that was when this small black cat showed up around here. It started following Ambrose wherever he went. Ambrose was terrified of this cat. He was so scared that he ordered Noah to follow him everywhere and protect him from the cat."

Stephanie burst out, "Protect him from a cat?"

Ben nodded. "You see, he was sure that the cat was trying to kill him."

"Cats can't kill anything—except rats and bugs and birds. That's ridiculous!" Stephanie scoffed.

"That's what everyone else thought, too," Ben said. "Except that one day, Ambrose was found lying dead in the courtyard beneath his bedroom window. He had fallen from it."

"How horrible!" Stephanie felt the hairs on the back of her neck rise.

"My great-grandfather had entered his bedroom just before Ambrose fell. The small black cat had leapt at Ambrose, who backed up to get away from it. He stumbled and—"

"Fell out the window!" Stephanie finished for him.

Ben nodded grimly. "But this is the part that's important. The cat that made Ambrose Chilleen fall to his death had *one green eye and one blue!*"

CHAPTER 11

"I don't believe it." Stephanie put down her rag and the polish. "I mean, this is some kind of joke, right?"

"I wish," Ben said quietly. "But it's really unusual for a cat to have one green eye and one blue."

"B-but," Stephanie stammered. "Ambrose Chilleen died over seventy years ago. The oldest cat on record lived to be only about thirty-five."

"I don't know, maybe this cat is a relative of that cat," Ben said as he screwed the lid on the saddle soap. "I didn't know any of this, Steph, until I went to my great-grandmother and told her I wanted to come to Chilleen Academy. My parents don't have much money, so I needed her help to come here. She said she'd help me out, but she felt I needed to know the family history."

"Does anyone here know who you are?" Stephanie asked.

Ben shook his head. "After my great-grandfather died, my great-grandmother changed her name to Smith and moved away with her baby daughter, my grandmother, to California. They started over fresh."

Stephanie let out a deep breath. "Whew! That's an amazing story. So do you think this cat's returned because you're here, Ben?"

Ben shrugged. "I've been here for nearly two years. Why did it wait till now? And why is it haunting my best friend instead of me?"

Then a possibility struck them.

"The charm!" they both exclaimed at once.

"And now I need to show you this," Ben said. He pulled two pieces of paper out of his pocket and unfolded them. One was the Xerox copy of Stephanie's hand. The other was a paper napkin with charcoal smudges on it.

When she peered closer at the napkin, Stephanie realized what Ben had been doing the night she followed him to the graveyard. He had used the napkin and charcoal to make a rubbing. It was a rubbing of the markings at the base of Ambrose Chilleen's tombstone.

"Check this out," Ben said.

He pointed to the Xerox copy of the scab on her hand. Stephanie looked at the symbol and then back at the tomb rubbing.

There was no mistaking it. The two symbols were identical.

CHAPTER 12

BEN spent the rest of the day trying to contact someone at a nearby college who could read Egyptian symbols. He didn't have any luck.

After dinner that night Stephanie left Laura in the dayroom playing Ping-Pong with Jane and went back up to her room. There was nothing more she could do. They weren't going to get any further with the mystery until they found out what the strange markings meant. Besides, she still had to study for that killer math test.

Once she was in her room, Stephanie checked under her bed, in the wardrobe, under her desk, and beneath the chair for the black cat. She was glad she didn't find it. Then she closed and locked the window. Stephanie was in no mood for uninvited visitors.

She flopped down on her bed and opened her math

book. After reading only a page and a half, she heard a sound.

She listened closely and made out a "meow."

The black cat was standing in the middle of the floor! She was carrying something in her teeth.

The cat leapt up onto the bed and laid the thing on the bedspread next to Stephanie. Then she moved back, seating herself gracefully, and watching Stephanie.

Stephanie remembered how her pet cat used to bring her little gifts. She'd be watching TV or reading a book when the cat would come in and lay something at her feet.

Sometimes it would be a dead mouse. Other times a dead mole. Or it would be nothing but a pile of feathers and a beak.

Stephanie knew it was one way a cat showed her love. She was always careful not to hurt its feelings by saying what she felt about the little presents, which was totally grossed out. At home she'd get a paper towel and flush the gift down the toilet.

This present on the bed wasn't a dead mouse, or a mole, or even a pile of feathers.

It was an odd, lumpy-looking thing—a little like a stuffed gym sock. Stephanie took her pencil and poked at it. A puff of dust came out.

Instantly the air was filled with the smell of incense, the incense from her dreams. This time she heard music, and the sound of human voices chanting in that harsh language. It had to be the language the ancient Egyptians spoke.

The voices droned on, growing louder. The sound filled her ears, blotting out her thoughts. The scent grew stronger, too.

Then she noticed another smell in the air—one that the incense only barely covered. It was a scent more powerful than all the oils and spices in the world. It was a scent she knew well. She had smelled it in the refrigerated room at her father's pet hospital and been sickened by it. It was the scent of death!

She was horrified to see that she was actually holding the thing that the odor came from. It was no larger than a girl's dancing slipper. With a sudden, sickening jolt, she realized what the thing was.

It was a foot. A small human foot, about the same size as Stephanie's. Only about five thousand years older. A mummified human foot.

She opened her mouth to scream, but no sound came out. Instead, she started losing consciousness. She was falling, falling backward into bottomless blackness.

CHAPTER 13

STEPHANIE opened her eyes and saw the foot in front of her. It wasn't on the bed any longer but on red, hard-packed earth, and she was lying flat on the ground near it.

She lifted her head and saw stone walls on which torches were mounted. The torches burned. She was in some sort of stone room.

The walls were beautifully decorated with symbols. There were strange pictures of men with hawks' heads. She saw pictures that were half-hippo and half-dog, half-cow and half-cat, and half-woman and half-cat. Her eyes raced over serpents and fish and men and knives. All told a story she longed to know.

There wasn't time to learn, she knew. She heard voices and chanting. People were coming!

The chanting grew louder, echoing off the walls.

The chanters appeared, all marching in a line toward her. She scrambled to her feet to get out of their way. No one seemed to see her, though.

They were all men, dressed in short skirts, their chests bare. They wore golden headdresses and heavy necklaces of gold. Each carried something different: a golden jewelry box, a plate heaped high with fruit, a jar of grain, a golden chair, a jewel-studded brush and comb set, and a small model of a ship carrying a tiny casket.

Stephanie recognized these objects from the pictures in the books she had read in the library. They were things that the Egyptians thought the dead would use in the afterlife.

Four more men were at the end of the line. They were carrying a beautifully painted casket lying on a stretcher of gold. The casket was small.

It was made for a child. Suddenly Stephanie knew it held the body of the princess, the princess with the cruel uncle.

Stephanie saw the cat woman lurking behind a pillar. She was watching with tear-filled eyes. As the casket passed close to her, she reached out to touch it. Just then a shadow fell across the casket. The cat woman pulled her hand back. It was the uncle!

The uncle stroked the casket fondly. He was smiling. His smile wasn't comforting, though. It was threatening.

Others entered the chamber. Some looked like servants, others like members of the court. Many of them cried. But none cried as much, as brokenheartedly, as the cat woman.

"So young," said one of the servants, a woman not much older than a girl. "She died so young. How tragic to be poisoned by a piece of spoiled fish!"

"That's not what I heard," Stephanie listened to a young man whisper. "I heard it wasn't an accident. I heard she was poisoned . . . on purpose."

Several people turned to stare at the uncle. He glared back at them, daring them to accuse him. The people did nothing—they were scared of him.

Stephanie wasn't scared, though. Stephanie knew the truth.

"You did it!" she screamed. "You murdered her!"

Suddenly the cat woman's arms rose above her head, and she pulled the long red gown around her. She shrank back into the form of the cat.

The cat spat and leapt at the uncle's throat. Slaves rushed to his rescue. They grabbed the cat and pulled her off him. He staggered, his chest bloody with scratches. The cat twisted in the slaves' arms, spitting and howling, her claws red with the murderer's blood.

Clutching his chest, the uncle commanded, "Kill it. Kill it now and bury it with her!"

Stephanie screamed and ran after the slaves. She

threw herself at them, trying to save the cat. They didn't notice, though.

"Oh, no! How did you get up there, Steph?"

Stephanie opened her eyes and looked down. Laura was standing in the doorway of their room, staring *up* at her.

Stephanie grabbed her head. She was so dizzy! The floor seemed so far away. Suddenly she realized that the floor *was* far away. She was crouched on top of a six-foot-tall clothes wardrobe.

How in the world had she gotten up there?

CHAPTER 14

"IT'S just like the Case of the Weight-Lifting Landlady!" Ben said. He, Laura, and Stephanie were sitting in the dayroom. Stephanie had finished telling Ben and Laura about her latest dream. Laura had just returned from the kitchen, where she got Stephanie something hot to drink.

"Here, drink this," Laura said, pushing the steaming cup of cocoa across the table to Stephanie. "What's a muscle-bound landlady have to do with Stephanie?"

"Well," Ben said, "it turned out this landlady had an ax murderer for a tenant."

"Wonderful," Laura said sarcastically.

"He was chasing her all over her house. Finally she managed to get in a room and lock the door so she could call the cops."

"Get to the point, Ben, please," Laura said.

77

"I'm getting there," Ben said. "The cops came and took the crazy tenant away. But they had to get a buzz saw and cut through the wall to get the landlady out of the room."

"How come?" Stephanie and Laura asked together.

"Because the landlady was so afraid of the tenant that she had shoved a two-thousand-pound safe up against the door. A one-hundred-pound little old lady moving a two-thousand-pound safe is pretty hard to believe, isn't it?"

Stephanie and Laura both nodded. Then Laura said, "I still don't get how this relates to what happened to Stephanie."

"Well, it was adrenaline that made it possible. It's a special chemical the body makes when it needs to protect itself. It's what helps athletes break world records. In your dream, Stephanie, you were trying to rescue the cat. In real life you actually jumped. The dream disappeared, and there you were, Steph, on top of that wardrobe. It was adrenaline that got you up there. I only wish I'd been there to see it."

Stephanie lifted the cup to her lips with trembling hands. The hot chocolate felt good going down.

"First the cat, then the dreams, then her fingernails, and now she can leap six feet straight up! This just keeps getting stranger and stranger," Laura said, her eyes behind the wire-rimmed glasses huge.

"I just wish I could do something," Stephanie said. "They need my help, the cat and the princess. And I feel like I let them down." Stephanie shook her head and took another sip of cocoa.

Laura reached out and gave Stephanie's arm a comforting pat.

"No offense," Ben said, "but there's really nothing you can do. If your vision is right, then the mean uncle poisoned his niece, the princess. Then he killed her cat. It happens to be about five thousand years too late for you to save either of them."

"Then what does she want? What does the cat woman want? Why is she haunting me?" Stephanie's voice rose.

"Well, Steph," Ben said, "you say the princess was wearing a necklace just like yours. Maybe your mother was wrong. Maybe yours isn't a copy. Maybe it's the real thing."

"And the cat wants to bring it back to her mistress?" Stephanie shuddered at the thought of some moldy old mummy wearing her necklace.

"Maybe that's what the cat meant when she said '*Return.*' As in, *Return my mistress's necklace*—or else? Hmmm," he said. "That gives me a brilliant idea." He snapped his fingers. "Why didn't I think of this before?"

Stephanie stared at him uneasily.

"Hey!" Ben exclaimed. "How can we get in touch with your mother? She must have one of those beeper gizmos. Doesn't she?"

Stephanie nodded. "The magazine usually knows where she is and how to reach her," she said. "Why?"

"We need to call Libby and ask her to get in touch with the shopkeeper who sold her the necklace. I'll bet he can tell us something about it. Or at last, tell us what the symbols on it mean. Then maybe we can find out what the cat woman wants."

"Great idea!" Laura said.

"No." Stephanie shook her head. "Not a great idea. Libby hates to be interrupted when she's on a hot story. I mean, *really* hates it—unless it's an absolute emergency," she finished stubbornly.

The other two stared at her in silence.

"And I suppose this isn't an emergency?" Ben said.

"No, it isn't," Stephanie said. "Long nails, weird dreams, and stray cats don't add up to an emergency."

Ben sighed. Laura just frowned at her roommate.

No one said anything. After a while Stephanie rose to go.

"I've still got to study for that math test, cat woman or no cat woman," she said. She left her two friends in the dayroom with their heads together whispering.

Stephanie awoke the next morning to the loud ringing of her alarm clock. Her hand shot out to click it off.

She stretched and stared up at the poster of the Persian cat on her ceiling. She smiled at it, feeling strangely peaceful. She had had a restful night of sleep, so maybe the visions were over. Maybe the cat woman had finished with her tale and was moving on.

"Hey, Laura." Stephanie rolled over and called out to her roommate.

Nobody answered.

Stephanie sat up and stared at Laura's bed. It was empty. It was already made—as if it had not been slept in the night before. Stephanie saw that the clothes that Laura had laid out the night before were still hanging over her desk chair. Laura must have never come to bed.

Stephanie got up and dressed quickly. She ran down to the dining hall, trying not to worry. Laura had merely slept on top of the covers, worn a different outfit, and gone down to an early breakfast, she told herself.

"Have you seen Laura?" she asked Jane.

Jane and Bridget were studying for a social studies test. The girls shook their heads.

"Not this morning," Jane said. "But I did see her last night. With Ben. She and Ben were walking across campus to the woods."

Toward the graveyard? Stephanie wondered. "Have you seen Ben?"

Jane shook her head.

Stephanie looked around for Ben. He was usually the first one down to breakfast and the last to leave. Ben wasn't at any of the tables.

Oh well, she told herself, *maybe he's at the stables.* He's probably eaten already.

She raced over to the stables, arriving there breathless. "Vernon, is Ben here?" she asked the stable hand.

Vernon shook his head as he sat on the corral fence, sipping a mug of coffee. "Nope," he said. "He isn't working this morning. He is this afternoon, though. When I see him, I'll tell him you were looking for him. How's your head? Giving you any trouble?" he asked.

She looked at Vernon as if he were crazy. Then she remembered her fall from the horse.

It seemed so long ago that Rusty had thrown her. "Fine," she told him, backing away. "Fine."

Her head wasn't fine, though. It was full of troubled thoughts. *Where were her two best friends?* It was too much of a coincidence that both of them should be missing at the same time.

She sat through English and social studies that morning not paying any attention to the lesson. In between classes she asked everyone she passed in the hall if they had seen Ben or Laura. No one had seen either of them since the day before.

Stephanie didn't know what to do. *Don't panic,* she told herself, taking deep, calming breaths. *Whatever you do, keep your head. There's got to be a logical explanation. It's a small campus, and they've got to be here somewhere, right? But where?*

By late morning she was really worried—and really jumpy. Science was the last place she wanted to be, but at least it was the last class before lunch.

When the teacher announced that Bobby Worth was going to be her partner for that week's lab experiment, Stephanie groaned.

"What's the matter, Cuddly Kitten?" Bobby nudged her. "Afraid of me?"

She gave him a dirty look as she poked her head through her lab apron and tied the strings around her waist. "Let's just do the experiment and get it over with, okay?" she said.

"The experiment's right up there on the board," Bobby said, smirking. "Why don't you read it to me, and I'll do the dirty work?"

Stephanie looked up at the board. In one column the teacher had listed the symbols for the chemicals they were supposed to use in the experiment. In the other column she had listed the amount of each chemical. As Stephanie studied them, the symbols began to swim before her eyes. They were grouping and regrouping themselves until they looked like . . . she couldn't believe this . . . hieroglyphs!

Stephanie shook her head. Maybe Vernon was right to ask about her head. Maybe it was giving her trouble. Maybe the fall had rattled her brains. Or affected her eyesight.

She rubbed her eyes.

"What's the matter, kitty cat? Your eyes getting tired from all that midnight prowling?" Bobby teased.

She scowled at him. "No, and if you don't mind, I think I'll do the experiment myself. Why don't you share with Kristy Michaels? I see she doesn't have a partner."

"Okay, kitty cat," he said, walking away.

Stephanie swallowed, then forced herself to look at the blackboard again. To her relief, she saw just plain ordinary chemical symbols. She set to work, measuring out the various chemicals.

She glanced up at the board to double-check the exact amount she was supposed to use.

Suddenly the chalked symbols began to move around again. They wriggled about on the blackboard like living things. Finally they resettled into four rows of ancient Egyptian symbols.

Stephanie bit her lower lip and looked around at the other students. Some of them were studying the board, but they obviously weren't seeing the same writing she was. The other students were quietly doing the experiment, laughing and talking with their partners. Everything appeared to be absolutely normal.

Stephanie felt totally alone. As she stared at this bunch of ancient symbols, she wondered if she was going crazy.

Her heart thudded in her chest. Blindly she reached for a measuring spoon, adding a pinch of this, a dash of that, a little water. She had to fake it. She had to do the experiment any old way. Maybe no one would notice she had no idea what she was doing.

Before long the classroom was filled with the scent of strong-smelling incense. The potion in Stephanie's test tube bubbled and boiled.

She raised her head from her work. All talking had stopped. Everyone was staring at her. Mrs. McGill, the teacher, came over and stood next to her.

"Stephanie Markson, what in the world are you up to?" the teacher asked as she bent and sniffed at the test tube. "Stephanie, you're supposed to be testing the acid level of the water. What you've got here smells more like perfume—or incense."

Stephanie dropped the test tube she was holding. It shattered on the floor at her feet. She backed away from the brew boiling away in the other test tube.

"I-I'm sorry, Mrs. M-McGill—" Stephanie stammered. "I guess I'm not feeling well today. It must have been the fall I took from a horse. I—"

She tore her apron off and ran out of the room. She needed to get away from that classroom and the horrible smell and the odor it was meant to cover up—the stench of the dead.

CHAPTER 15

AFTER lunch Stephanie had to shovel out the entire stables, doing Ben's job as well as hers. Neither of her friends had shown up yet. They had been missing for over twelve hours, and she was really worried.

Mrs. Danita had come looking for Stephanie that morning, asking why Laura wasn't in class. Stephanie had been quick to cover for her and said Laura was sick in bed.

Now Stephanie knew that that had been a mistake. She shouldn't have lied. It would have been better to tell Mrs. Danita the truth, that both Laura and Ben were gone without a trace.

As soon as she was finished, she decided to report both of them missing. The police would come and start asking all sorts of questions. Stephanie swallowed the lump in her throat. She'd just have to answer their questions as best she could, leaving out the dreams and the charm and—just about everything. Somehow, she knew they wouldn't believe her.

She was nearly finished forking down fresh hay from the loft when the tack room telephone rang. Vernon was out doing errands. Hoping it might be Ben or Laura, she scrambled down the ladder to answer it.

She picked up the phone, her heart pounding. "Hello?"

"Steph, is that you?" The connection was crackling, but there was no mistaking that voice.

"Mom?" Stephanie said. She sat down hard on a nearby saddle. She couldn't believe it was her mother on the phone. It was such a relief that she nearly cried. "How are you? How's the whale story?" she blurted out.

"Okay, but it sounds like you and your friends are onto an even better one. Are Laura and Ben with you?" Libby asked.

Stephanie realized that Ben and Laura *had* called her mother last night, after all!

"No, they're—" Stephanie started to tell her, but Libby broke in.

"Never mind. I'm sure you want this information as much as they do, so here goes: I managed to get in touch with the shopkeeper in Egypt. I faxed him the same Egyptian symbol Ben faxed me last night."

Ben had actually faxed her mother? There was a fax machine in the *Canyon Echo* office, and Laura had the key.

"It turns out the symbol isn't a word. It's a name. It's the name Sakarra, a young Egyptian princess who lived about five thousand years ago. She was murdered by her uncle. The charm I gave you is a copy of one she supposedly was wearing when she was buried," Libby explained.

Stephanie leapt to her feet. *Sakarra!* So now the princess of her dreams had a name. She was real!

"Anything else?" Stephanie asked.

"Yes, I had a friend in Egypt look up the Clancy tour that Ambrose Chilleen paid for. Well, this was the exact same trip on which they discovered the tomb of Princess Sakarra. Interesting, eh?"

Stephanie gulped. *Very interesting,* she thought.

Libby went on. "The tour caused *quite* a scandal, it seems. The tomb of the princess was vandalized."

"Someone stole the jewels?"

"No. Someone stole the *entire tomb*, Stephanie, stone for stone. It was a small tomb, but still—the Egyptian government was really upset. Clancy and his crew left under a cloud of suspicion."

"Did they ever find who stole the tomb?" Stephanie asked.

"No, but one of the guards at the site confessed twenty years later on his deathbed."

"Confessed to stealing the tomb?" Stephanie asked.

"No, confessed to taking a bribe to look the other way as the tomb was taken apart. Guess who gave him the bribe, honey? Your own Ambrose Chilleen. Isn't that exciting? Ambrose Chilleen must have stolen the tomb! Aren't you just dying to know where he put that tomb? Honey? Stephanie, are you still there?" Libby asked.

Stephanie was no longer listening to her mother. She was staring at the open window of the tack room. The cat woman was crawling through the window! Stephanie screamed and dropped the phone.

"Return!" the woman hissed.

The smell of incense stung Stephanie's nostrils.

She gasped and grabbed the first thing she could lay her hands on—a riding crop.

The cat woman moved toward her slowly. Her arms were raised over her head. Her nails dripped with blood!

CHAPTER 16

STEPHANIE screamed and backed away.

"Stay away from me!" She snapped the crop wildly in the air.

The cat woman was making a rumbling sound back in her throat, half-purr, half-roar. She came closer and closer.

Stephanie raised the crop, but was unable to hit at the woman.

Now the cat woman was about three steps away. Stephanie sobbed and flung the crop aside. Then she turned and ran out of the tack room into the stable yard.

"*Return!*" the cat woman snarled. She raced after Stephanie, her claws dripping blood. "*Return!*" she shouted again.

Stephanie took off across the yard and ran toward

the woods. She ran as she had never run in her life, because she was running for her life.

Stephanie had no idea how far she ran through the woods with the cat woman steps behind her.

Sometimes she was lucky and hit upon a path. Except for roots and fallen branches, the going would be easier now.

Then suddenly, up ahead, in the middle of the path, the cat woman appeared.

"*Return!*" she screeched, racing at Stephanie.

Stephanie dodged her and ran into the thick woods. Branches slapped and stung her cheeks and snagged her hair. Burrs clung to her pants and socks, poking through the fabric and rubbing her skin raw. Birds and other small creatures scattered before her as she crashed through their homes.

Stephanie tripped over a root and fell heavily to the ground. She struggled to get up. Leaning forward, hands on her knees, Stephanie tried to catch her breath.

Then she felt a strange sensation. Something sharp and cold was crawling up her back.

She swung around. The cat woman was standing over her, scratching her with her nails!

"*Return!*" the creature hissed.

With a scream, Stephanie shook her off and ran deeper into the woods. She didn't care where she ended up. All she knew was that the cat woman wanted to hurt her, and she had to outrun her to survive.

Even as she ran, though, she knew it was useless. The cat woman could appear beside her at any time.

Finally, after running until she thought her lungs would burst, Stephanie broke into what seemed to be an open field.

It was no field. It was the Chilleen family cemetery.

She paused, to get her bearings. She was standing on the far side of the cemetery. The quickest way back to campus—to help—was directly through the middle of the graveyard.

She swallowed hard and tried to calm herself. She had to do it. If she went the long way, or went back into the woods, the cat woman might be waiting for her.

She began picking her way through the wild and weedy cemetery. It was an obstacle course. Waiting to trip her were old grave markers, dried-up arrangements of flowers, bushes and sagebrush, snake holes, and who knew what else? She stumbled onward.

"*Hoot-hoo!*" came a noise from above her.

Stephanie froze. It was only an owl, probably the same owl she had heard the last time she was there. She continued on, faster now. She was halfway through the cemetery.

A mass of storm clouds moved across the sky, blocking the sun. She heard thunder rumbling not far off. Then she heard "*Yip-yip-yeee!*"

This time she didn't stop. She told herself that it was only coyotes.

At least, she tried to cheer herself, the cat woman seemed to have disappeared. It had been quite some time since Stephanie had seen her. Perhaps she had gotten lost in the woods. Stephanie hoped so.

Stephanie was passing the monument of Ambrose Chilleen when she heard an ear-piercing screech that made her blood run cold. The cat woman might be gone, but the cat was back.

It was perched atop the statue of Ambrose Chilleen. The cat's fangs were needle-sharp and glistening. Her muscles were tight. She was ready to pounce.

Stephanie pressed herself up against the front of Chilleen's tombstone, hoping to protect her face and neck from the creature's sharp teeth and claws. She covered the back of her head and neck with her arm, and tensed for the attack.

Then she heard them: faint but clear voices.

They were crying out, from deep under the earth— and they were calling Stephanie's name!

CHAPTER 17

LIGHTNING flashed across the sky. She stared up at the statue of Ambrose Chilleen. The cat was gone!

Again the voices cried out. There was no mistaking them. They were Ben and Laura, and they needed her help.

Another flash of lightning lit up the sky. In that brief instant Stephanie saw the small, lighter-colored panel on the bottom of the marble marker. The hieroglyphic symbol was carved there. In that instant she knew where Princess Sakarra was buried. In a hidden chamber beneath her feet. That was the mysterious secret project Ambrose Chilleen had been working on in the woods!

Her heart hammering, Stephanie knelt down and touched the ancient symbol. She leaned against the stone with the weight of her entire body.

She heard a harsh grating sound. The stone was moving!

A doorway about eight feet wide opened up in the marble tomb. Ambrose Chilleen's gravestone had a secret panel that hid the tomb.

She peered into the doorway. A set of steep stone stairs led down. Ben and Laura's shouts were clearer now. They were trapped down in the tomb!

Wishing she had a flashlight, Stephanie started slowly down the stairs.

As she reached the seventh step, something or someone pushed her from behind. She lost her balance and fell, plunging into pitch blackness.

CHAPTER 18

*A*S Stephanie fell, the smell of incense filled her nostrils. She knew it meant that she was about to have another dream.

Once again she was in the Egyptian stone room. She saw the same pictures on the walls. The odd creatures, half-hippo and half-dog, half-cow and half cat, half-woman and half-cat. Serpents and fish and men and knives—all told a story she longed to know.

Then she looked down at the pounded earth floor. It wasn't red as before, she noticed. Suddenly it struck her. She wasn't in ancient Egypt. She was here—now—at Chilleen!

The cat woman stood before her.

"Who are you?" Stephanie asked.

"I am the ghost of Princess Sakarra's cat," the cat woman replied.

"How did you get here?" Stephanie asked, backing away.

"When my mistress was murdered by her uncle, I was drowned in the Nile, mummified, and buried with her. For thousands of years we lay peacefully side by side in her small tomb. Then one day men came and broke into the tomb, disturbing our sleep.

"At first all they did was fuss over us. They cleaned us off with brushes and made lists in their notebooks of my mistress's treasures."

"That would be Clancy and his assistants," Stephanie said.

"But then the one with the beard—"

"Ambrose Chilleen," Stephanie said.

"I hate his very name!" the cat woman spat. "He paid thugs to steal us for himself and smuggle us out of Egypt. When he finally had us to himself, he had workmen reconstruct our tomb, here beneath the ground, where no one would ever find us.

"He used to come down here by himself and gloat over his treasure. But one day he was carrying my casket across the room and he tripped. He dropped my casket and it cracked. He didn't know it at the time, but he set my spirit loose, to haunt him!

"And haunt him I did, from that day onward. I followed his every move. I, a tiny, harmless little black cat, drove him to the brink of madness. And death!

"Ever since that day, I have walked the Chilleen estate, in search of someone who would help us return to our land. I had nearly given up hope when you came. You were wearing a necklace just like the one around my mistress's neck. That was wonderful enough. But you also had a power beyond this. You had the power to understand animals and to sympathize with our suffering. I knew in my heart from the moment I saw you that you were our only hope."

Then the cat woman was silent. She waited for Stephanie to answer. But what could she say? "I can't help you," she tried to explain. "I'm as powerless as Sakarra was. I'm just a kid. I'm not even a princess. . . ." Stephanie's voice trailed off.

The cat woman stiffened. Whirling around, she spat, "Very well, if you cannot help us, you will be buried alive with us!"

The cat woman scrambled over to a wooden mallet, and picked it up. She walked over to the wall where a clay knob was sticking out.

Lifting the mallet over her head, she brought it down on the knob with a mighty whack. The knob shattered, leaving a hole in the wall.

IN THE MUMMY'S TOMB

A stream of pale red sand began pouring into the room.

Stephanie watched helplessly as the cat woman continued walking along, cracking open more knobs. Four streams of sand now came pouring into the room.

CHAPTER 19

"I T'S about time you found us!" Ben's voice cried out, bringing Stephanie back from her dreamworld. She opened her eyes to see burning torches along the walls, and Ben and Laura running into the room from a tunnel off to one side.

Stephanie rubbed her eyes to look around the room. In the center was a large stone platform. Lying on top of it was the beautiful casket of the Princess Sakarra.

Off in the corner a smaller casket stood. Stephanie knew instantly what it was. It was shaped like a cat, a black cat. Its eyes, one green and one blue, were made of precious gems, one emerald and one sapphire.

Then Stephanie noticed something else. The casket

was cracked wide enough for a cat to have slipped out. And it was empty!

"Stephanie, please snap out of it and help us get out of here." It was Laura pleading with her now.

Stephanie blinked and studied her two friends. They looked terrible. Their faces were smudged and pale, but at least they were alive!

Stephanie reached out and hugged them both. "I've been so worried about you two! How did you get down here?" she asked.

"Last night—" Ben said.

"After we faxed your mother," Laura interrupted, guiltily. "I didn't want to fax her, but Ben insisted."

"That's okay, I forgive you," Stephanie said. "She called you back today, and I got the message. Lucky for you that I did, too. But I'll tell you about it later. Go on."

"We were just coming out of the newspaper office," Ben continued with their story, "when we saw the little black cat in the hallway."

Laura started talking. "I wanted to run get you, but Ben was so excited, he started following it. The next thing we knew, we had followed it all the way to the graveyard, to Ambrose's gravestone. Then the cat just kind of vanished! Ben was calling it, and I was leaning against the gravestone, trying to catch my breath, when suddenly—"

"The tomb opened up!" Ben finished excitedly. "Revealing a hidden passage!"

"Laura must have leaned on the panel with the Egyptian marking," Stephanie said, thinking out loud.

"Anyway, we climbed down. The next thing we knew, the door slammed shut and we were trapped down here. Ben says he figures this is an exact copy of an Egyptian tomb."

"It's no copy," Stephanie said. "It's the real thing." She went on to tell them all that Libby had told her about the vandalism of the tomb of Princess Sakarra.

"Fantastic!" Ben said. "Ambrose Chilleen was a tomb robber. Mystery solved!"

"Except," Laura said, "for the mystery of how to get us out of here. Thank goodness Ben had a pocket flashlight. We've been exploring some of these passages, trying to find a way out. So far, no luck."

"There are about nine tunnels, but they don't lead anywhere but back into this main room," Ben said.

"What about the stairway, the way we all got in?" Stephanie asked.

"No good," Ben said. "That automatically locks. Any other ideas?"

Laura turned her head and cupped one hand to her ear. "What's that noise? You guys hear it?" she asked.

"What noise?" Stephanie and Ben asked.

"Kind of a whooshing sound," she said.

Even before they saw the sand piling up on their feet, Stephanie knew what it was. Her dream—it was coming true. Sand was pouring into the tomb from four separate holes in the walls. They had been so busy talking, they hadn't even noticed the sand rushing into the tomb.

"Someone's trying to bury us alive!" Ben screamed.

CHAPTER 20

BEN pulled off his shirt, then his socks. He used them to try to plug up the sand holes. The force of the sand only pushed the clothing out, though.

"Maybe there's some kind of turn-off switch hidden around here," Laura said. She had to raise her voice to be heard over the sound of the sand.

Laura and Ben started groping along the walls in search of a switch. By now the sand was up to their ankles.

"Stephanie, don't just stand there! Help us!" Ben shouted.

Stephanie felt numb. "This is all my fault," she said miserably.

"Look, this is no time to feel sorry for yourself!" Ben shouted. "Do something. Shout for help! Take a rock and beat out an SOS. Do *something!*"

Stephanie shook her head sadly. "She begged me. The cat woman begged me to help her, but I told her I couldn't."

"Told *who* you couldn't?" Ben paused in the middle of trying to shovel the sand over to one corner using his shoe.

"I told the cat woman I couldn't help her! In the last dream I had. I told her that I was just a kid and there wasn't anything I could do! I guess that was a dumb thing to do," she said.

Ben was shoveling and didn't answer.

Stephanie shuffled through the sand and knelt before the cat's empty casket. She had to talk to the cat woman again.

There were now about six inches of sand on the floor. It was pouring in so fast that soon there would be a foot. Then two feet. Eventually it would fill the main chamber and tunnels and cover their chins, their mouths, and their eyes. Then they would smother.

"I'm sorry," Stephanie said to the empty casket. "I'm sorry that I said that now, kitty. I really am. I understand now what you wanted."

The sand would pour in and bury them, and she'd never see her mother or her father or her home again. She lifted the collar of her shirt to wipe the tears off her face.

When she looked back down at the casket, she saw the cat slithering out of it. The cat then jumped into her lap.

Ben and Laura were now shoveling sand together, trying to keep one small area clear of sand. They were too busy to even notice what Stephanie was doing.

She felt the cat, soft and warm in her lap. She heard its purring. The cat stared up into Stephanie's eyes.

"You wanted me to help you and your mistress," Stephanie said. "And I promise I will help you if you get us out of here alive. I'll go to Mrs. Danita. I'll go to my mother. I'll go to her boss. I'll go to the president of the United States himself, if that's what it takes!"

The cat purred and rubbed its face against Stephanie's hand.

"I'll make sure the whole world knows the terrible thing that's been done to you. They'll know that you've been dishonored, kidnapped, and held prisoner thousands of miles from your home," Stephanie exclaimed.

"Then I'll make sure that they pack you up and take you back home to Egypt, where you belong!"

Stephanie looked around. The sand was now almost up to her lap. It was falling faster. So were her tears. The cat's fur was soaked with them.

"But, kitty, I can't help you if I'm buried beneath a million tons of sand. So help me. Help me and my friends get out of here alive, and I'll help you. I swear," she pleaded.

Stephanie lifted up the charm and kissed it. "I swear to you on the necklace of your mistress, the Princess Sakarra."

The cat climbed out of Stephanie's lap and padded over to the entrance of one of the tunnels. She stood and waited for Stephanie to get up and wade through the sand after her. It was hard going.

At the first bend in the tunnel there was a giant statue. It had the head of a dog and body of a hippo. It was sitting on its tail, and its four stout legs stuck out like four large pegs.

The cat leapt up onto the statue and rubbed against the legs of the hippo. They looked like corks for giant wine bottles. *Corks!*

Stephanie felt an almost electric jolt as she realized what they could be used for.

"Laura! Ben! Get in here!" she screamed.

Ben and Laura pushed through the sand to the tunnel. "What are you doing here, Stephanie?" Ben shouted, annoyed. "We already tried this tunnel. It's a dead end!"

"Help me pull off this hippo's legs," she shouted back. She must have yelled awfully loud, because both of them obeyed her instantly.

The corklike legs popped right out of their sockets. They were heavy but not hard to carry.

"Use these to plug up the holes," Stephanie directed.

She took one under each arm. Ben and Laura each took one. Together they pushed through the knee-deep sand back into the main room. It was like carrying firewood through a snowdrift. Stephanie's legs and arms ached from the strain.

Again Stephanie shouted over the roar of the rushing sand. Her throat was beginning to feel raw. "You take the hole on the far wall, Ben! Laura, you do the one nearest here! When you're done, come back and help me with the last one! Hurry."

They nodded, knowing as well as she did that they didn't have much time. Once the sand covered their arms, they'd be helpless!

They managed to stuff all four plugs into the holes. Slowly the roar of the sand died down until at last all was silent.

They fell back into the mounds of sand to catch their breath.

Then they sat up again and looked at one another. One by one, they burst into laughter.

Their sweat had made the sand stick to their skin. They were coated in it!

"We look like human sugar doughnuts," Ben said.

"Don't say that," Laura groaned, "you're making me hungry!" They laughed and then a frown covered Laura's face. "It's great we stopped the sand," she said. "But we still have no way to get out of here. We're trapped!"

CHAPTER 21

SUDDENLY Stephanie heard the cat meow. She saw the black creature on a high platform under the princess's casket. The cat pounced on a stone knob carved in the shape of the sun.

Over her head Stephanie heard the harsh grating sound of stone against stone. The sound was like music to her ears.

The smells of the outdoors—of earth and pine needles dampened by rain—came rushing down the stairs. They all lifted their heads to the stairs and the opening and drank in the fresh air.

Then Ben said, "Let's get out of here."

"I'll second that," said Laura.

"Wait," said Stephanie. She made her way over to the corner where the cat's casket lay buried now beneath the sand. Carefully she swept the sand aside. The other two came over and helped her dig it up.

When the casket was unearthed, Stephanie said, "Here, kitty, kitty."

The little black cat, who was still sitting on her mistress's casket, leapt down.

"You're one very tired kitty cat, aren't you?" she said. "All you want to do is curl up in your casket and sleep. That's all you've ever wanted to do, isn't it, kitty cat?"

The cat meowed and leapt into the casket like an obedient modern-day cat climbing into her traveling box.

Purring, the cat made herself comfortable and closed her eyes.

Gently Stephanie gave her one last pat on the head and fit the lid onto the bottom.

"Phew!" Ben said. "Good work. Now let's get out of here before something else strange happens."

"I think I should bring her with us," Stephanie said. "As proof."

"Good idea," Ben said. "Let's go."

Ben was the first to make it to the top of the tomb's stairs. He called back to the others. "Look out! It's pouring rain up here!"

Stephanie took off her jacket and carefully wrapped it around the cat's casket.

They made a dash up into the pouring rain, Stephanie hugging the casket to her chest. She heard a noise that drowned out the thunder of the storm then. It was ten times louder and much more menacing.

For a minute Stephanie was sure that it was the guardians of the dead coming to get them for opening the tomb of Sakarra.

Then Stephanie looked up. Bright spotlights blinded her. An enormous black shadow hovered in the air. They were going to be taken away!

Then she saw it was a helicopter.

"Thank goodness you're all right!" a voice called out over a megaphone. It was Libby!

Never in her entire life was Stephanie ever so glad to see her mother.

"Stephanie Markson," Libby called out, "pardon a mother for saying this, but you look like something the cat dragged in."

Stephanie's hair was tangled and matted. Her clothes were torn, ragged, and filthy from her mad dash through the woods. Grains of wet sand still covered her. Stephanie grinned. She didn't care. She was going to save the cat and princess. With Libby's help, of course.

Stephanie, Laura, and Libby were sitting at a table in the dayroom, the cat's casket on the table in front of them.

"After you screamed and dropped the phone, I really panicked," Libby said. "I called the school from Seattle, but the line was busy. So I tore down here as fast as I could. It took a private jet, a private plane, and a helicoptor, but I made it! I must say, it was worth it. This is one terrific story."

They had taken turns filling Libby in on their adventure. When they got to the part about the tomb, Libby started looking just a bit doubtful.

"You mean to say that this cat saved your lives?" she asked.

"She was very clever, wasn't she, Steph?" Ben said.

"Open the casket and introduce your mother," Laura said to Stephanie. "She's still in there. Stephanie coaxed her in before we left the tomb. She's probably still asleep. Go ahead, Steph, open it up and show your mother the world's cleverest cat."

Stephanie carefully lifted off the lid of the casket.

Everyone gasped. There in the casket lay the shriveled mummy of a cat who had died five thousand years ago.

EPILOGUE

TWO weeks later Stephanie was in the stable feeding Rusty a lump of sugar when she heard the padding of sneakers across the stable yard.

Moments later Laura Hobbes poked her head over the stall door. "You'll never guess what came in the mail today!" she exclaimed.

"What'd you get?" Stephanie asked, backing out of the stall and closing the door.

"My mother's banana nut bread. Flat as a pancake and smells delicious. Want some?" Laura asked.

"You bet," Stephanie said.

"Oh, and something else came," Laura added. "This month's copy of *Coaster* magazine."

Stephanie's face lit up like the Fourth of July. She grabbed the magazine out of Laura's hand and read the headline on the cover aloud. "Students Rescue

Five-Thousand-Year-Old Mummy. Egyptian Government Reclaims Rightful Property."

"Let's read it," Stephanie said.

She and Laura read the article as they walked back to the dorm. In the magazine's glossy color pages were photographs of the caskets, those of Princess Sakarra and her little pet cat, staring out at them like old friends.

Egyptian archaeologists were busy even now putting the tomb back together, the article said. They would be returning the princess and cat to the tomb within a few months. In the meantime, they were being kept in a climate-controlled room. Thanks to the dryness of the southwestern climate, little damage had been done to the mummies.

Back in their dorm room, Stephanie got out her scissors.

"What are you doing to my magazine?" Laura wanted to know.

"Don't worry, I told my mother to send us a dozen copies. But this one, I'm cutting up," Stephanie said.

She snipped out the photograph of the cat casket and pinned it to the bulletin board next to the other cat pictures. She stood back and looked at it approvingly.

Laura took what was left of the magazine. "Before you slice this to ribbons, I'm going to show it to Ben. *If* you don't mind."

"Be my guest." Stephanie smiled.

"Are you coming with me?" Laura asked.

Stephanie nodded. "I'll be there in a minute, Laura."

When her friend had gone, Stephanie stared at the bulletin board. There was no doubt about it—she missed that little black cat. She had gotten used to having it around. Stephanie reached automatically for the Egyptian charm, but it wasn't around her neck. She hadn't worn it since she was in the tomb.

Suddenly she felt like wearing it again. Maybe wearing it was the next best thing to having the cat around.

She went over to her jewelry box and opened it. It was lying in the top tray where she had left it two weeks ago. It looked different now, though.

It was the same green stone with the markings carved into it. But now, mounted in the center of the stone, was a beautiful yellow gem, a topaz.

Stephanie took it out and held it up. It glittered in the sunlight, golden yellow. It was a topaz, all right. There was no doubt about it. A cat's-eye topaz.

She smiled to herself as she went to the mirror to put it on.

About the Author

LYNN BEACH was born in El Paso, Texas, and grew up in Tucson, Arizona. She is the author of many fiction and non-fiction books for adults and children.

Coming next—

Phantom Valley™

THE HEADLESS GHOST

(Coming in December 1992)

Jenna, Rob, Deidre, and Jeff desperately want to be members of the Shadow Club. But getting into this popular club means going into a spooky old cabin filled with bats and surviving a terrifying initiation. And then they must confront the feared headless ghost! There's something strange and very scary going on in the Shadow Club. The four friends wonder if belonging to this club is worth risking their lives!